I0576354

Shady Woods

Book 1 of the Shady Woods series

J Mercer

Published 2020 / Bare Ink

Printed in the United States of America

Print ISBN: 978-1-7348883-2-4

E-ISBN: 9781734888317

Library of Congress Control Number: TXu002221752

SHADY WOODS / written by J Mercer

Cover design by Bare Ink

Copy edits by Aurielle Destiche

Contents

Chapter 1

Master It, Hide It, Keep It

You coming, Grace? my brother asked from the screen door, with only a thought reaching out from his brain to mine.

My dog and I were sprawled on the lawn, like we were about to make snow angels. Only it was September, and the first day of school in a town without one normal human being, when normal was all I'd ever known and all I'd spent my life trying to be.

My mom stood behind my brother, her nervous face on. If there was one thing I couldn't stand, it was when the nervous face threw itself down for the disappointed one. Disappointed, usually, with my obstinance, which was a word I'd learned at a very young age.

1

My brother disappeared down the hallway, so I got up and hurried inside. I'd definitely get the disappointed face if I fought this school thing. Whether or not I wanted this high school, or this town, when the nasty words I'd thought of that stuck-up cashier slipped out of my mind and into hers, I'd sealed my fate.

Master it, hide it, keep it—that was our mantra. I'd lost control only once, but two weeks later we were here, where they would teach me what I couldn't teach myself.

Following my brother through the house, I let my mom flutter around me with a perfume of worry, fingering through my hair while trying not to look like she was fixing anything, and squeezing my shoulders because she knew I didn't want to be hugged.

She knew I wasn't going to fit in here. And she should know better than anyone, since this was where she'd grown up. My dad, too. They'd left for college and raised us like normals, wanting us to have the experience of living mainstream, because, and I quote, "there's more to this world than just the small sect of abnormal culture."

*Ab*normal, which was short for "above normal." Though, if you asked me, the culture was "below normal" since it hid beneath ordinary society.

It had to hide. Chaos would result if it didn't. If *we* didn't.

Individually, we might have the upper hand over the humans, but there were so many more of them than there were of us. And they wouldn't be happy with us roaming free. To them, we'd be monsters, even if that's not how we saw ourselves. I mean, sure,

2

someday I'd be able to shock people with my fingertips and push thoughts on someone's brain, but mostly I was harmless.

We all were. At least, those of us who were pacifists, like the ones in Shady Woods. Weird place though. Cut into a forest and nestled against Shady Bay, nothing but nature loomed for miles in any direction. It was the opposite of Chicago, where I'd grown up, but a better place for people like me.

Dendrites like me. There, I said it. I was a dendrite.

My parents had let me live normal, then ripped me out and stuffed me into this small hole inside of nowhere northern Wisconsin. But like trying to fit something back in its packaging after it's been out, we all knew it wasn't going to work.

Only four years, I reminded myself. Then I'd go to college with the friends I'd just left and never look back.

Justin was halfway to the sidewalk, so I looked at Zeus, also wary (dogs always knew), buried my face in his blond and white mottled fur for good luck, then hurried after my brother.

In Chicago the sidewalks were anything but sprawling. And wrought iron fences lined the townhouse properties, instead of the hedges they seemed to prefer here.

I walked with my eyes closed so I could pretend I was walking my old neighborhood with my best friend Charlie, the way this day was supposed to have gone. Until I about tripped over a curb. Then I pouted the rest of the way. It didn't take long.

Stopping in front of the one-story brick building, I shook my head. "I still can't believe this is it."

"This is it," Justin said, shoving me along from behind.

"It's the size of a little kid's school."

"It's quaint, you mean?"

Three guys were lounging on the grass like they were in no hurry for the first day of school, either. One kid, who I'll just call Legs, had a long piece of grass sticking out of his mouth like he was about to wrangle some pigs. What self-respecting vampire walked around with grass in his mouth?

The squatty block of a werewolf next to him nodded at us as we passed, and the reasonably human-looking dude with the tattered baseball cap I was going to guess was dendrite, like me.

Ignoring them, I marched my way into the school to the blue freshman wing where I'd found my locker the day before. Of course, this time there were people standing in front of it. Three of them, and I tried not to stare, but they were nearly identical, with varying shades of the same chestnut-colored hair and pretty much the same face.

After a slow, tedious beat, the short one stuck her hand out. "Hi, I'm Ava. You must be the new girl." She was built like a gymnast. But in this world, short and muscular meant wolf, not gymnast.

I shifted my notebooks to my other arm to shake her hand. "Grace James."

"Riah Jenkins," the boy with Ava's face said. "Like Ryan, but without the N."

The face looked better on him, but he had some seriously hairy arms. He wasn't quite as beefy as your average male wolf, though. Not as squat, either.

The third could only be a vampire, tall and stretched out like pulled taffy. While she had the same features, they looked like they'd been squished between a door.

"I'm Maribel," Squishy Face said. "Nice to meet you."

"What's your first class?" Riah asked.

"Um..." Shuffling the armful of crap I was holding, I found my schedule, which had been on top of the pile a minute ago. "History/civics."

"Me, too." He closed his locker. "I'll show you where it is."

I about snorted when it was just across the hall and three doors down from our lockers. So terribly hard to find.

We had alphabetically assigned seats, so Riah ended up behind me. Mrs. Smith, a vampire with hair to her waist, sat cross-legged on the front of her tidy desk, hands bracing the edge. Thin, rectangular glasses hung from her neck by a beaded string. Ivory collared shirt buttoned to the top. Black pencil skirt with a vicious slit up the side. And red-hot platform heels. Like the top half of her belonged to someone else than the bottom half.

As she droned on about her plans for the year, I paged through the bulky text that was waiting for us as we'd entered the room: *The Way We Live—A Look at Four Diverse Governing Bodies.* It was written like fiction and drawn like a fairy tale, so if any normal stumbled on it, that's all they'd take it for.

It hit me, then, that I was about to become a character in a book. After four years of imprisonment here, would my friends even recognize me when I went back? Or would they only see a girl who'd once been real, colored like a character out of a story?

———

It was third period English when my existence was publicly announced.

The teacher's beady eyes settled on me almost immediately, like I was a splinter he was trying to root out. There was nothing to do in the face of that kind of stare but raise my brow. *What?* is what a raised eyebrow said.

His face did not flicker. But then, he was clearly a vampire, and vampires are the epitome of calm, cool, and collected. To a fault.

I heard epitome a lot as a kid, too. As in, "That daughter of yours is the epitome of obstinate."

Mr. Jacobsen did not flicker in the face of my raised eyebrow. He simply said, "Well now, a new face. Grace James, is it? Please stand."

Stand? I wanted to ignore him and deny being the new girl, because everyone watched the new girl. But his attention, and all the stares that it pulled in my direction, prodded me up like branding irons. Charlie had always stayed in front of me at center stage. That was how I preferred it.

"It's been awhile since Shady has welcomed anyone new." He pressed his fingertips together, letting them bend further than a normal would be able to.

With a wince, I looked away to find a particularly interesting guy a few seats over from me. Tousled black hair, relaxed but intent face. Not as eager and bubbly as the rest of them. Lips turned up in the smallest hint of a smile.

I smiled back at him as Mr. Jacobsen instructed me to tell the class a bit about myself.

A bit about myself?

Apparently, I was taking too long, because the girl next to me poked me with her pen.

I tore myself from the cute boy to focus. "Um, I'm Grace, from Chicago. My parents grew up here, and I have a dog." *I have a dog?*

The girl next to me snickered, as did a number of others, and I shrunk slowly back to my seat. Not such a smooth city girl now, was I?

I have a dog? The girl wrote. **You're funny**.

I closed my eyes and waited for Mr. Jacobsen to start his lecture. When I opened them, she was tapping her short, painted fingernails on her notebook, where she'd added: **I'm Stella Clark.**

She was tall and slender (sleek, more than stretched out), with strawberry-blond hair and pale, moonlit blue eyes. Scattered flecks of silver glinted from her irises.

I was polished, I knew how to do that, but every one of these sirens was beautiful. Exquisite. Formed by an artist. Graceful in a way that couldn't be taught.

When the bell rang, she leaned over the aisle and I felt the tug of her charm, her personal magnetic pull. "Nice to meet you, Grace James," she said, her voice smooth as silk. Then she peeked at my schedule. "I have gym next too. I'll show you how to get there."

Following her out of class, I failed to point out that I'd had the school mapped in five minutes. But whatever. I could hear my mom's voice in my head, reminding me to be open to new friends.

"We don't really do pets around here," Stella said, once we hit the hall with the white lockers.

"Why not?"

"They're for normals. They're a normal thing." She wrinkled her delicate nose just slightly. So slightly, I was guessing she didn't even know she'd done it.

"There's nothing wrong with normals," I snapped. Normals were my people.

She raised her brow at me in a totally different way than I just had. It said *Chill out.* "I'm not saying there is. I'm just saying it's a human tradition. I mean, sirens are water mammals—have you ever seen a whale with a pet? And werewolves eat small animals as an appetizer. Not to mention, if a vampire had one around, they'd be using its blood for something important."

I made a face, not liking the idea of a vampire using Zeus's blood for anything, important or not. She grinned and threw an arm around my shoulder, like we were friends already. I frowned.

"Animals around here have a purpose, you know? They're not for cuddles."

"Well, Zeus *is* for cuddles."

She dropped her arm and laughed, pushing me forward into the locker room as if we'd known each other for years. Then she changed into gym clothes in front of me like we'd known each other even longer than that.

As soon as we hit the gymnasium, she linked arms with a vampire, whispered something in his ear, then looked over her shoulder at me.

"This is Ethan. He's my boyfriend. We'll sit with him and his best friend Riah at lunch."

I bit my tongue from saying "We will?" because where else would I sit? And anyway, I'd already met Riah. I mean, how many Riahs could there be?

Ethan held a spindly hand out as I caught up to them. "Nice to meet you, Grace." His speech was languid—not like a southern accent, but like he operated at his own, relaxed pace.

I ignored his hand. He shrugged and dropped it. Never would I get used to the soft body of a vampire. They were a whole lot less bone than the rest of us. A whole lot more cartilage and tissue, which meant they were super flexible and kind of squishy.

Shivers.

9

A sturdy female werewolf marched in front of the bleachers we were gathered on. She introduced herself as our gym teacher and went into a speech about the importance of stretching. It was so important, she said, that it was all we were going to do today. And, she promised, it would start and end every one of our classes.

When she released us, we grouped in little circles on the floor. Of course, now that Stella thought she could herd me around, I ended up with her and Ethan.

"What are dogs for, Ethan?" Stella asked, as she threw one arm over her head in a perfect arc.

"They're an aphrodisiac," he said, folding himself over his legs and pressing his cheek to the side of his calf. "Love juice."

It was disturbing. I could hardly look at him. "They're man's best friend," I corrected.

"She *is* human," he said, bending his neck at a weird angle to look at Stella. My stomach rolled.

"That's what they're saying about you," Stella said. "But don't worry about it. They just had to find *something* to say."

"Why would I care if they're saying I'm human?"

Now Ethan was doing that bendy neck thing in *my* direction. I folded forward, squeezing my eyes shut.

"We're neighbors, by the way," Ethan said. "I saw you guys moving in. Saw that tasty dog." Stella must have slapped him. That's what it sounded like, and then he chuckled. "Kidding! Kidding."

I didn't say anything, didn't move, just held my stretch and my breath. Maybe if I passed out on the first day of school my parents would send me back to Chicago.

"She told everyone in English she has a dog," Stella said with a loud laugh. It was a beautiful sound. Like a wind chime, but not an annoying one.

Ethan snickered. "New girl bringing the love juice on the first day."

I snapped up rigid.

"Calm down," Ethan put a hand up. "We got your back."

"I don't need you to have my back."

Then they shared a look, like they knew something I didn't.

Chapter 2

I Have a Dog

I knew plenty, and I was still grumbling about it as I sat down with them at lunch.

I knew plenty about them and their way of life, along with a whole lot more that they didn't have a clue about. They stayed in this little town one-hundred percent of their life to keep normals safe and oblivious, but I'd done so much more. And I wasn't done doing it, either. I'd be gone to live again as soon as my four years here were up, because I had plans: college with Charlie in Arizona, studying abroad in Italy with Charlie and Matteo, then I'd be a nurse—Rea too—and we'd all move to some beach town with a big city, because Allie always said big cities on the ocean were the best of all worlds.

They didn't have plans, and they didn't know anything. They knew nothing about me and what I knew, at least. So who were they to judge?

I crushed a grape between my teeth as Stella took a spoon to a can of tuna. Dry tuna, seaweed, and four bottles of water.

The bench gave a little under me as Riah sat down on my side of the table. Yep, same guy—lean body heavily dusted with Mountain Man fur. That was going to take some getting used to.

With a light smile, he pulled out his sandwich. I eyed it.

"Turkey." He nodded. "Just like yours."

I about snorted. Mine was politely oven-roasted instead of raw, pink chunks. Taking a big bite, Riah ripped open his brown bag to reveal two more sandwiches, and Stella started chugging water.

As Riah's sisters walked by with little waves to sit at the next table, it occurred to me that as easily as Riah could be a wolf, he could also be a hairy dendrite.

Except, could three different abnormals come from two parents? I guess if one of his parents was a mix... Okay, fine, so I didn't know much about their genetics, and that was kind of interesting.

"What are you?" I asked him. "What are your parents?"

He cocked his head before he answered. "A wolf, like my dad, just with my mom's vampire genes to stretch me out."

That explained the raw meat. It was a wolf thing. Duh. Maybe I'd spoken too soon.

"Do I get to ask you a rude question now?" he asked.

"How was that rude?"

"*What are you?* You don't think that's rude? What are *you*, huh?"

"I'm a city girl."

"You're a dendrite. Only, you're embarrassed about it." He chewed and swallowed, his burnished brown eyes on mine. "So, what? You tried to pretend you weren't one back in Chicago?"

"There was only one thing to be back in Chicago."

"So that's why you're all choked up with despair?"

"I'm not—"

"Don't bother. I can smell it."

"Excuse me?"

"I can smell it. Wolves can smell emotions, you know."

Well, of course I knew that. Except it had never been my reality before. I shifted in my seat. "Everyone can smell my despair?"

"Well, it smells an awful lot like diva, which is the game you're playing, so I wouldn't worry too much about it."

My short laugh surprised both of us. "I guess we're even, then," I said.

"Even how?"

"Rude for rude."

He grinned and went back to his sandwich, leaving me feeling totally off-balance, like he could see directly inside me.

No one could do that, though, not even me. Dendrites couldn't hear anyone's thoughts but their own, couldn't rifle around unnoticed in another's head, like a telepath could. Or like they couldn't, since they didn't exist. We existed, dendrites, and all we could do was project, with the strength of our mind, onto another's senses.

"So what's Chicago like?" Stella asked.

"Awesome." I bit into my sandwich, then added, "Like my dog."

"You have a dog?" Riah asked.

"Yes. And he's for cuddling."

Ethan chuckled and Stella told Riah, "She's funny." Then, to me, "You're funny."

"This place is funny," I muttered.

Riah looked around, thoughtfully. "This place is better than your Chicago."

I rolled my eyes.

"Diva," he muttered. But when I shot a look to him, I could tell he'd been joking because he was almost smiling. That made it a little better.

"So what do you like to do, besides cuddle pharmaceuticals?" Ethan asked.

The grape between my fingers popped. I wiped the juice off on my napkin, and replied, "I like to try new foods, and go new places, and experience new things, and see new shows, and discover new music."

"Then what's your problem with Shady Woods?"

"There's nothing new here."

"To you, it's *all* new," Riah pointed out.

"I've been here thirteen times already. Every Christmas to see my grandparents and aunt. It's not so new."

"Have you been to Parrino's?" Stella asked. "Or Al's? Or the Bluegill's Perch? Have you been to the beach—"

"Yes, I've been to the beach. And I've eaten Parrino's pizza. And I don't like freshwater fish."

"You need to lighten up," Ethan added.

"This place is magic, Grace." Stella whispered, tone soft. "Most people *never* get to see magic."

"Magic?" I echoed. "Have any of you ever been to a city?"

They shook their heads. That's what I thought. With a sigh, I decided to let it drop. I didn't want to argue with them about the merits of Shady Woods. They couldn't understand what they were missing.

"Why are you here then?" Riah asked. "If you hate it so much?"

"Why do you think?"

"Parents?" Stella asked.

Sure, let them think that. Better than the fact that I screwed up in the normal world, letting a thought escape. It *was* my parents, anyway. I'd told them it wouldn't happen again, that I'd figure it out. But they decided it was a transgression bad enough to send me to an abnormal high school.

Seemed a bit extreme, grounding me to this weird place for four years over one little word sneaking into someone's mind. But they had refused to compromise. That was the problem with parents, though, wasn't it? They teach you to compromise, but they're not so hot on it themselves.

My last hour was dendrite skills.

So fine, I was a little intrigued by this. As much as I'd wanted to be normal back in normal world, playing with my mind sort of made me feel like a superhero.

Mr. Turner, who I had earlier for algebra, nodded at me as I walked in. Then the guy from English, with the blue eyes and small hint of a smile, sat down next to me.

"I'm Christian. Christian Riley," he said, eyes glinting like Stella's did.

In the stories my mom told me when I was growing up, the mermaids cried shining silver tears. I knew better than Charlie how much truth was in her "made up" fairy tales, so I wasn't surprised by the silver flecks shining from every siren iris around here. But it was still something to actually see up close. When we came for Christmas all those times, we pretty much just stayed at my grandparents' house.

I swiped my bangs out of my eyes and tucked them behind my ear. "I'm Grace."

"I know. The one with the dog."

"Don't you like dogs?" I challenged.

"I've never really spent much time with one. It was just an odd thing to say about yourself."

Great. Now I was officially dealing in love juice. "It's not odd to me. He's my pet, and I was raised normal, and I love him." Why was I explaining myself to this guy? Because his voice was like cotton candy, soft and fluffy and delicious?

His amused smirk, which he seemed to run around with on a regular basis, grew a little. Then the bell rang.

"Good afternoon, class. Welcome to dendrite skills." Mr. Turner's plaid pants were tight on his thighs, and his crisp, white tee was covered with a vest. "If you'll please open the books on your desk to the second chapter, we'll get started." He was a pacer, and he paced the front of the room until all our books were opened.

"You'll see it talks about which skills you might have started to exhibit in the last year or so, as this is about when the neural pathways that allow you to communicate in this way fully mature." He clicked on the projector. "Who has experienced any of these?"

Signs of Dendrite Readiness
-Headaches created by excess energy
-Temples burning and throbbing
-Fingertips sensitive to the point of discomfort
-Intentional or unintentional remarks reaching intended target or unknown subject

Almost all of us raised our hands. Even me, though I hated to admit it.

"That's what I thought." He grinned. "For homework tonight, I'd like you to read chapter one, which goes into the mechanics of your ability, and chapter two, which describes signs of readiness. However, for class today we'll skip right to chapter three and try our hand at branching our minds." Scanning the room, he found me in the very last seat of the very last row. "Grace, would you like to start? Just a few paragraphs, and then we'll wind along the room."

I did as he asked, then read ahead as someone else took over. It said the prime situation for communication would happen when you were physically close to your subject and looking directly in their eyes. It listed suggestions for concentration and how to center your brain on the one thought you were trying to get across. You had to mean it and deliberately push it out there. The whole chapter was on this first step, branching one word to another person.

"All right." Mr. Turner's voice pulled my attention back. "Now, grab a partner and give it a shot. Remember to face each other, look into each other's eyes, and hold hands. One word only, no need to get fancy. Go."

"Grace?" Christian was already facing me, his hands hanging in the space between us.

I was confident, in general, but this branching was one thing I'd been avoiding for a very long time. I didn't have much practice and his face was curling my stomach in a very distracting way. I tried to shake it off as I slid my hands against his. They were warm, smooth, and thankfully dry. "You first," I said.

The fidgety room slid to silence, and soon it was so still that you could hear the tick of the clock and the click of Mr. Turner's pointy boots as he wandered the room.

I waited.

One minute.

Two minutes.

Three minutes.

Five.

"How long is this supposed to take?" the girl in front of us whispered. She was shushed by a handful of people, but Christian and I didn't move.

Another eight minutes. Good, so maybe I wasn't behind.

There were more mumbles and Mr. Turner reminded us to keep concentrating.

Seven more minutes, and a few people began to murmur with excitement.

Was my brain not empty enough? Would he be able to break in if it wasn't? I mean, I'm sure I wasn't the only one whose parents showed up in their mind without invitation, so how long would it take for us to be able to do that?

Four more minutes and the word *lovely* resonated softly in my head, in his voice. And that was beyond freaking cool. Plus, I'll admit, I melted a little.

Whatever was happening on my face must have given it away, because his lips curled up on one side. And he might have winked at me.

He could not have just winked at me. Did he actually just wink at me? Lovely was a pretty darn good word, but to follow it with a *wink*?

He shook my hand a twitch. "Your turn."

Yeah, he was pretty proud of himself. How about *cocky*, Christian Riley? How about there's a word for you.

Voiding my brain and putting everything I had behind it—all the irritation from this strange town and its weird people, the confusion I felt from being both intrigued with this silly brain crap while still wanting my world to flip back to normal—all of that emotion I redirected into energy, into force. I threw it behind that word, filled myself with it, then shoved it out at him, until my mind was again silent.

He burst out laughing. I dropped his hands.

"You're cute, Gracie. I'll definitely give you that."

"It's Grace," I corrected. And what a downhill slide, from lovely to cute. Cute was for bunnies. I frowned. Was he so arrogant he thought it funny that I just called him cocky?

He opened his mouth, but Mr. Turner stepped between us and put a finger to his lips. Christian's eyes shimmered toward mine and he held his hands back out, like he was going to send me something else. Then the bell rang.

We grabbed our stuff and walked out of class side by side. When it seemed like he was planning to walk me to my locker, I glanced over at him.

"How is it, being the new girl?" he asked. Cue another arrogant smirk.

"It has its moments," I replied. "Is that your normal smile?"

"Maybe, why?" He frowned. "What's wrong with it?"

"It's cocky."

The frown broke. "Some say it's charming."

"Who? Your mother?"

That's when I saw the full extent of his grin, as big and genuine as it got, the moment before laughter took over. It was beautiful, nothing conceited about it. I wondered how it was different exactly. Not as lopsided, I didn't think. And not like he was laughing at you, but like he was truly amused.

Fine, so both versions were kind of hot.

Shaking my head as we reached my locker, I asked, "What are you doing after school?"

His face immediately went slack. "Oh, I..."

What had *lovely* meant then? What had walking me back to my locker meant? I turned and yanked the door open. Stupid small town boys. Trying to be direct and then backpedalling like a baby. Whatever.

Hoping he'd be gone by the time I turned around, I packed up what I needed to take home, slowly zipped my backpack, threw it on my shoulder, put on some lip gloss, closed and locked my locker, then spun back around.

He was still there, but not saying anything, his forehead bunched a little, making him look confused. I about shoved past him when a spaghetti noodle of a girl draped herself over his shoulder.

She had silky black hair that fell halfway down her back and eyes dark as the devil. Her eyes, nose, and lips were all on the large side, and yet somehow her face itself still came off as angular. It worked, though. She was the kind of striking beauty you couldn't be unless your features were a little extreme.

Watching me, she kissed Christian on the cheek. "You must be the new girl," she said. "Very boring, girl-next-door. I would've expected more from a big city."

I crossed my arms. For as obstinate as I'd always been told I was, I'd also been told I looked sweet. Girl next door I'd gotten too, and vanilla. But boring was a first.

"Grace James, Sofia Hoffmann. Sofia Hoffmann,"—Christian gestured vaguely between the two of us, not looking either of us in the eye—"Grace James."

I almost wished I had a sixth toe now, something I could pull out and shove in her stupid face. Or a tattoo.

She tried to pull him away, but his arm was all that went with her.

"It was really nice to meet you, Grace," he said.

"No, it wasn't," she said, trying again, tugging on his hand. That seemed to shake him out of whatever daze he was in, and he sort of pushed her away from me, maybe because he was embarrassed she'd say such a thing.

He should be. I was embarrassed for him, that he'd pick a girl like that just because she was gorgeous.

Chapter 3

She Thinks She's Normal

"This is what we do after school." Stella was trying to convince me to come over to Ethan's with the three of them. She hung back on the sidewalk while Riah and Ethan headed up the walkway to his house. I glanced next door at our kitchen windows and decided it would be a lonely afternoon if all I had to look forward to was a phone call from Charlie.

Except I didn't want to be paired with Riah.

"Riah's too hairy for me," I whispered.

"I heard that!" he shouted, as Ethan pulled open the wrought iron door.

"And I'm bringing my dog."

Stella raised an eyebrow.

Throwing my arms up, I repeated, "I'm bringing my dog." Marching up to my house, I dropped my backpack in the front hall, yelled to my mom that I'd be next door, and motioned for Zeus to join me in the front yard.

They were still waiting for me, right where I'd left them, as if speaking of my dog had turned them into stone. When Zeus and I were halfway across the lawn, my mom stepped onto our front porch.

"How was school?" she asked.

I turned around briefly, but she wasn't looking at me. She was eyeing my new friends—if you could call them that. "Fine," I replied.

"Be home for dinner."

"Always."

Zeus was as obedient as dogs came and pretty much worked as an extension of me. So when I stopped next to Stella, he sat down at my side. The three of them stared at him.

I smirked. "You guys scared of a domesticated animal?"

Ethan laughed a little, Riah rolled his eyes, and Stella said, "I just don't know what to do with him."

"You'll figure it out," I assured, motioning for Ethan to head inside already.

"My dad might not like this," he muttered, pushing open the faded red storm door.

The little front foyer led into a long hallway with the living room on the left. Unlike my mom's windows, which were always dressed with sheers, theirs were covered with thick, eggplant-colored drapes. A man was reclined in front of a mumbling television, his eyes closed, and the noise of a women singing softly drifted down the stairs on my right.

At the back of the house, the kitchen was a shade brighter. Ethan went straight for the fridge, which was mostly lined with neatly ordered half-gallons of blood. Only one shelf held normal food, and I wondered who that was for.

"His stepmom," Riah whispered in my ear.

I shot him a look. Was he always going to know what I was thinking?

He leaned back and shrugged. "You smell curious. And were staring at the carrots. His stepmom is a dendrite, and his little sister."

Ethan grabbed a jug and took a couple of swigs, then headed for a door that was missing a few strips of wood at the bottom. We followed him down creaky stairs to the basement—to worn furniture, a large TV, and bookshelves of dust-coated DVDs. Riah and Ethan each slumped down on a couch, and I wandered to the back wall where a ledge was lined with framed photos.

Portraits and family shots varied from color to black and white, some so old they were cracked and yellowing. The sleeping man upstairs had obviously lived a really long life, seeing as he was the one common denominator.

Zeus was nosing my leg and looking at me like he wasn't sure what we were doing here. I scratched him behind his ear, not very sure myself.

The hackles on his marbled blond coat were up, and he was waiting for my lead, so I sat down in the stiff armchair that looked legit Victorian. Definitely not the most comfortable, but it was that, pairing myself with Riah on the couch, or squeezing onto the love seat with Stella and Ethan.

Zeus sat next to me, raised his ears at Ethan, moved over a foot, sniffed in Riah's direction, then leapt onto the couch next to him.

"Um…" Riah held his hands up as Zeus snuck his head onto Riah's lap, one paw resting over his thigh.

"Just go with it," I suggested.

Awkwardly, he patted Zeus' side a few times, before finally letting his hand settle. Stella and Ethan were pretty much snuggled together in the same way.

"How long have you been together?" I asked.

"I've known Ethan since kindergarten," Riah answered.

Stella rolled her eyes. "She's not talking to you."

Riah wasn't easy to read, but he was smirking like he'd known exactly what I'd meant. "She's been around for a year and a half. You have a boyfriend back home?"

I tilted my head. "I already said you're too hairy for me."

"Yeah, well, don't worry. You're too snobby for me."

"*Me* snobby, it's you who can't handle my dog."

"Hey, I'm handling him."

"He does seem to like you."

"He's a good judge of character, obviously."

"Or maybe you remind him of himself."

That shut him up. But we were both amused, I could tell.

Speaking of, "That nose of yours? It's like knowing what people are thinking."

"Pretty much, so don't think you can put anything past me."

I nearly snorted, having already gotten that impression. "Can you smell anyone?" I asked. "At anytime?"

"It helps if you know the person well enough that you can pull out their non-emotive aroma. So sometimes it's harder with strangers, but you're really easy to read."

"Great." Just what I needed.

"What the hell is that?" came a voice from the stairs. A voice as cracked and yellowing as the photos on the ledge.

"A dog," I answered, seeing as no one else did.

The man from the recliner took a few more steps and glanced between me and Ethan. "What the hell is a dog doing in my house?"

"She thinks she's normal," Ethan answered.

I narrowed my eyes at him and crossed my arms. There was nothing wrong with being normal, or thinking you were.

"She's the new girl, next door," Riah explained. "They do pets."

"He won't bite," I said.

"He better not, or I'll bite him back."

Ethan groaned. "Gross, Dad."

"Oh, geez. That's not what I meant. Anyway, how do you think you came to be? Think a stork dropped you off?"

Ethan put his hands over his ears. "Lalalalalala."

"He's very well behaved," I promised, eyeing Riah. "As long as no one tries to eat him."

Mr. Parrino looked down at the bottom step, then pointed at the pile of old LPs on top of the DVD shelves. "Ethan, grab me my *Doors* album over there."

"You're scared of him," I realized, as Ethan reached the cabinet.

"Hardly." But he snatched the album from Ethan like he wasn't going to step foot on the same floor my dog had been on.

I laughed.

"Get out." And he pointed up the stairs behind him.

No one was looking at me, except for Ethan's dad. Stella was playing with the hem of her shirt, Ethan was studying the floor like it was suddenly very interesting, and Riah was really paying attention to Zeus.

"What?" I asked him.

"I'm not some newfangled, feel-good dad who thinks kids are cute. I think they need to be polite, to everyone. Got it?"

Suddenly, there was a huge lump of hairy rat in my throat. I tried to clear it.

"Get out now and maybe I'll give you another chance tomorrow."

He didn't move. I didn't move. Riah was smirking a bit, but still petting Zeus like they were long lost friends. Stella looked kind of sad, and Ethan was staying out of it. I guess they looked like kids who knew better than to cross him. Or be anywhere close to "not polite."

Wait. Was he serious?

"You have five minutes." Then he turned and went back up the stairs.

It was quiet for a long, uncomfortable moment, then Riah stood. "Come on, I'll walk you home."

I looked up at him, slightly in shock.

"I know, I know. I'm too hairy for you. I'll still walk you home."

Zeus was waiting at his side, clearly anxious to get out of there, so I guess there wasn't much left to do, but try again tomorrow.

⸺⁓⸺

"I can't believe we'll be here for the carnival this year," my mom gushed at dinner.

Gushing was suddenly her new thing. She gushed over being back, and doing this again, and that, and now this stupid carnival.

"I prefer Halloween," my brother said. The carnival was on the first day of November, so we'd been told not to expect a Halloween.

"You have no idea," she said to us. "It's not what you think. It's like all the holidays wrapped up in one."

"Great!" Justin grinned. "So we get presents in November *and* December?"

"No," my grandma said with a snort. "It's like Halloween with Fourth of July fireworks and a Thanksgiving parade—"

"But no parade, just the throwing of candy," Grandpa interjected.

"And Easter for the kids, because the next morning there's a hunt for all the candy left hiding in the grass and bushes." My mom clapped her hands together once. "Oh! And you forgot New Year's, with the kissing during the firework's finale, instead of at midnight!"

I gave my dad a look, like, can you believe this giddy wife of yours? Where did she come from? Also, what kind of Frankenstein holiday was this carnival anyway?

He winked at me. "It's been exactly seventeen years since we've been. I'm pretty dang excited about it too."

"Well, I'm not excited. You know why? Because I got kicked out of the neighbor's house." I shoved a bite of steak in my mouth and chewed it hard. "So that's how my day one went."

My brother snickered.

"Because I'm too normal," I added, with a sneer, in his direction.

"Or because you're a brat," Justin said. "Because you don't know when to keep your mouth shut."

I shifted in my seat and poked at the misshapen glob of mashed potatoes on my plate. "Ethan's dad doesn't like dogs."

"You brought a dog to a vampire's house?" my grandpa asked, fork halfway to his mouth.

"So?"

My dad went to loosen his tie like he usually did halfway through dinner, but he didn't wear a tie anymore. Accountants here didn't dress as formally as they did at the big Chicago firms. "This place is different, Grace. You have to be respectful."

"How was I supposed to know that wasn't respectful?"

"I told you there wasn't a vet in town," my mom said. "I warned you when we brought him."

"You warned me that if he got sick, there might not be anything we could do. And that he wouldn't be able to get his shots, and that they weren't used to pets around here. You didn't tell me everyone would hate him."

She gave me a look—that infuriating *are you listening to yourself?* look.

"Fine."

"What did Mr. Parrino say exactly?" my grandma asked, knowing every person who lived in every house on every block. "He's rigid, but he's not irrational."

"Oh, he's irrational," I mumbled through a small mouthful of mashed potatoes.

"What did he say?" she asked.

"He said I could have one more chance, if I left right then."

This sent Justin nearly slapping his knee with glee, so I pinched him, hard.

"Not at the dinner table, Grace," my mom warned. Then she burst out with an inappropriate laugh and a smile for my dad, as if he'd just said something in her head.

I narrowed my eyes at them. There was that, too, in addition to the gushing. Ever since we'd gotten here, they'd been all about the secret, silent exchanges. It hadn't been something that happened back home. And when the four of them did it—my grandparents too—it was creepy. All those facial expressions and laughter with no words? Unnatural. As if they'd already forgotten where we'd come from.

How could they just revert back to something they weren't? Or, at least, something I'd never known them to be.

It was like sliding across shifting rock, when you felt like you didn't know your parents anymore.

For example, Riah's mom had been over that afternoon when I got home from Ethan's. A vampire, who'd always been a vampire, who'd apparently also been my mom's best friend in grade school. Imagine that. My gentle mom with the motherly flutters, who could hardly squish a worm beneath her heel, all bestie-bestie with a blood-sucking vampire.

My mom had her pre-dinner coffee while her old best friend enjoyed a steaming cup of blood. Which my mom had provided.

Now we were the family with a half gallon of blood in our fridge for guests.

I fisted my hand around my fork.

My dad's eyes shot from my hand to my face, as if something I'd been thinking had escaped. I pressed my fingers to my temples and tried to think about strawberries, polar bears, and other favorite things, in order to hopefully better control my thoughts.

My dad was waiting for some swear word to accidentally pop into his mind. He knew enough to know that whatever I was thinking, he wouldn't approve of. This was sort of like saying it anyway, but it was a game we played for the sake of practice with the outer world. If I could keep it from slipping out of my head and into his, he wouldn't hold it against me.

I slid one knuckle up against a nostril and took a deep breath in, then out. It was a yoga breath, a calming breath, from when Charlie and I went with our moms to yoga on Saturday mornings.

There was no yoga here. No *namaste*. No *shanti*. No finding a place to center.

I dropped my fork back to my food, and my dad went back to the conversation.

"Yes, the entire back corner of our lot."

"That's ridiculous!" my mom cried. "Who would start a fire in the woods in the middle of the night?"

My grandpa shook his head. "Some stupid kids." And he punctuated this with a glance across the table to me and my brother, a gentle reminder that he thought all kids were stupid.

"What were they aiming for?" my dad wondered.

37

My grandma sighed. "If it had reached the fields, it would have spread like wildfire."

"Amy said someone started a fire at the movie theater last week," my mom said. "Out in the trash area. It singed the corner of the building but was put out before it did any real damage."

I rolled my eyes. Amy was Riah's mom.

"What's happened here?" my dad asked. "It used to be so pleasant."

"Everything's pleasant when you're a kid," Grandma said.

Even with the talk of arson, my mom was nearly giddy as she cleared the table. Again, she'd never before been the giddy type. She was a mom, for goodness sake.

With a grin, she wrapped her arms around my grandpa's neck and kissed his head. He patted her hand, and she stood to bring another load to the sink. Grandma got up to help her, and they laughed, their heads bent together in silent conversation.

I pushed away from the table and marched across the hall to the living room.

It was almost a duplicate to the one we'd left behind. The over-stuffed couch, huge armchair, and coffee table were arranged in front of the fireplace. The sheers on the windows had come with, the lamps, artwork, pottery—all recognizable. Differences were slight: a brick mantle instead of wood, and traditional beveled corners instead of the blunt, rough edges on the trim that lined our last home.

As my dad and grandpa filed in to watch the news, I wondered what I was doing here. I had homework, and I didn't really want to talk to anybody. I didn't want to hang out all night with family I didn't even know anymore.

It was bad enough I had to start a new school in a new place, twice as bad that it was really a whole new world, and three times as bad that my own parents weren't who I'd always thought them to be.

The only good news was that I couldn't see it getting any worse.

Chapter 4

Purist Nonsense

A car door swung open in front of me, and I almost slammed into it. Ethan, who I'd walked to school with, grabbed my arm and pulled me back while I stared the guy down—the werewolf from the front lawn yesterday. He watched me, took his time getting out, then turned to catch up with Legs and his other friend, both of whom had gotten out on the other side.

"Those guys are bad news," Ethan said.

"What kind of bad news?"

"They skip school and, well, mainly they leave town."

I squinted my eyes at him. "That's it?"

"That's it?" He shuddered. "Leaving town puts us all at risk, Grace. If anyone followed them back…"

I considered this. It would explain why we came back so little, only once a year, but it also made me feel more locked up than I did already. "Wait, are you telling me that's as bad as it gets around here? Like, what about stealing and doing drugs?"

Opening the front door of the school for me, he very seriously replied, "Who would steal and do drugs?"

"Oh! What about those vandals?"

"I doubt that's a kid." He put a hand on my arm as I brushed past him. "And you should take that purist nonsense seriously."

Smirking, I pointed at him. "You just told me to take nonsense seriously."

"*Purist* nonsense," he stressed, while walking backward toward his locker.

I didn't know what that meant, so I headed to history to ask Riah. Only, he was already asleep at his desk. On the second day of school.

"Oh, never mind," I muttered, flipping open my book. I could not get enough of the pictures—especially in the siren monarchy chapter we'd had to read for homework. Octopi and seahorses were too cool.

Mrs. Smith diagrammed everything I'd read last night, answered any questions we had, and told us what to read for tomorrow. It was pretty easy, considering sirens were naturally the most peaceful of all of us and didn't need much governing. They had a king as a figurehead and security only for when he went on land; done and done.

"Well, good morning," I said, as the bell rang and Riah stood to join me.

"What'd I miss?"

"Please, as if I'm helping you. You just slept through the second day of class."

"Surprise, surprise," he drawled, in a tone very unsurprised. "Our little diva doesn't believe in helping others."

I hugged my books tight to my chest as we swung into the hall. "I help others."

"Not much of a sharer, then?"

"Ugh. Fine. We went over the reading and are supposed to do chapter two for tomorrow." I flung the door of my locker open and threw my stuff inside.

He laughed his way over to his. "My dad's in politics, Grace. He's on the town council. I've known this stuff since before we started school."

I gave him a look.

"But you are insanely fun to tease."

"I thought we were supposed to be friends." Were we, though? I'd done nothing but complain yesterday.

They had time for me, at least, unlike my real friends back home. When I'd tried to call Charlie last night, she didn't answer and texted me instead, but only for a few minutes, as if our entire lives together meant nothing and I didn't need that familiarity so bad it physically hurt.

I thought about it during algebra, and by the time Stella glided over to my locker with her yellow English notebook, I'd decided it might be worth making nice, even though she was pointing to the word English, which was scripted in huge silver block letters that seemed to sparkle, like I was stupid and needed help remembering my schedule.

If my old familiar wasn't going to come through for me, then maybe I could find some new familiar.

I grabbed what I needed, then realized I'd forgotten to ask Riah what "purist nonsense" meant. I asked Stella instead.

"Purist nonsense?" she repeated. "I don't know what you mean."

"Well, I obviously don't know what I mean either. Ethan was just saying I should take it seriously. Which, well, do you see the irony?"

"There's no irony there. You *should* take it seriously."

I stopped in the doorway and turned to face her. "*What* should I take seriously?"

"Purist nonsense, of course." And past me she went to settle into her seat.

"Right." I slapped my notebook down on my desk. "Let's pretend I'm in kindergarten, and you're telling me about purist nonsense for the first time."

"Oh." Her mouth held that shape for a moment. Then, relaxing, she said, "I'm not sure I want to be the one to tell you about that."

"Why not?"

Christian walked between us, cutting short our conversation. He continued behind me and up the next aisle, then sat down next to me on the other side.

44

Stella's eyes widened as Christian leaned toward me and offered up a shy smile. "Hey, Gracie."

"I think somebody's already sitting there," I said. Though shy smile was better than the arrogant smirk from yesterday, he'd still been a complete idiot.

I did not do complete idiots.

Turning toward Stella, I added, "You know, wasn't, um, who was that?"

She grinned, apparently more interested in how this was going to play out than how I felt about it.

Okay, maybe I deserved that. Note to self: Start acting like a friend. It did not escape me that this was the third time today I would have preferred a friendlier response.

Christian ran a hand through his short, perfectly messy hair, and said, "I'm sorry about yesterday."

"You should be."

"I just wanted to welcome you to the school. I didn't mean to give you the wrong impression."

Tilting my head at him I wondered if that's really all it had been. Had I jumped to conclusions? I guess it had only been like an hour before I'd assumed he'd say yes to a sort of first date. Maybe I should be apologizing for putting him in a tight spot, seeing as I hadn't even checked to see if he had a girlfriend in the first place.

I ran my hands over my face. This was not me, these were not my people, and I obviously didn't know how to act or what to believe. Maybe lovely meant something else here. Maybe he'd been looking outside, and had meant it was lovely out there, not that I was lovely, sitting in front of him. Maybe I needed to stop thinking I could read these people like I could read people back home.

"I want us to be friends," he added, looking down at the floor between us. "If for nothing else, then because we're skills partners."

I breathed out. "Okay."

He grinned, that full smile again, the one I liked best. "Okay?"

I nodded. "But you have got to stop calling me Gracie."

Stella, with a flourish, scribbled out, **What is going on?!?**

I ignored her. Christian straightened up in his seat and tried to get a look at it. She snatched it to her chest, but throughout the hour, whenever she'd catch my eye, she'd lay it back out and point to the words. As soon as class was over and Christian was out of sight, she clutched my arm and started begging, "Please, please, please," over and over, the whole way to the locker room.

Thankfully, she didn't bother me about it in front of Ethan, and then we were at lunch.

Assuming I'd be safe there, I relaxed. Until Ethan started gagging.

"Grace!" he cried, between bouts.

"What?" I cried back, as he held his nose with both hands. "Holy crap, what?"

"Are you trying to kill me?" he mumbled, from beneath his palms.

I put my hands up and looked at them, then at the table, then to Ethan. "What are you talking about?"

Riah flipped over one of my garlic crackers, which I liked most with cheddar cheese.

"Oh, give me a break. You cannot be for real right now."

Stella turned on me, indignant. "Surely you know that garlic kills vampires."

"But it's not raw. It's in a *cracker*. And it's three feet away from him." Plus, he had to ingest it for it to do any damage.

"It stinks." He shuddered. "It really, really stinks."

I was definitely getting more looks than I had yesterday. Why wouldn't my mom have warned me when I was packing my lunch? Though, she had been a little preoccupied with grilling my brother about the girl he'd spent all night on the phone with.

I kept screwing up, and my brother already had a girlfriend. Go figure.

Slumping my shoulders, I scooped the crackers into my empty bag and stood to toss it in the nearest trash. But that didn't seem to appease them. Everyone who'd been staring was still staring, and now some heads were shaking too.

With a sigh, I dug the bag out of the garbage and marched out the back doors, which led to the parking lot, figuring I'd drop it in the trash can there. But it was already overflowing, and a couple who were making out stopped to stare at me. One of them curled their lip up in disgust, revealing a fang, and though I'm sure it was about the smell and not about me, exactly, I went rushing off around the corner to another, less-used door, and dropped it in the trash can there.

Once back at the lunch table, I apologized. "How can I make it up to you?"

"Your blood, for starters, wouldn't hurt."

Holding still, I forced myself not to gape at Ethan. He had to be kidding. He did. That's what the wink meant, right?

Then again, everything seemed backwards here.

My new friends, if you could call them that, erupted with laughter, and I shoved a square of cheese in my mouth.

"Don't worry, Grace. You're too fresh. I'm not used to that kind of tasty goodness."

I didn't know how old the stuff from the blood bank was, but I knew he drank it on the way to school, like coffee. I also knew there might be some of me soon in his mug, since my mom had made an appointment for me this weekend at the blood bank. "They need a constant supply," she'd said, "and only dendrites can provide that for them."

"Grace James, right?" said a voice from behind me. Riah stopped chewing, Ethan half-raised an eyebrow, and Stella stopped drinking, water bottle still pressed against her lips.

I turned to find the smiling face of a tall vampire, which I suppose was redundant, but wow, was he tall. "Look, I'm sorry," I said. "I didn't know, and I threw them out."

48

"Oh, I'm not here about those crackers—though, you might've had us all retching if you hadn't."

"I'm new at this," I admitted. "But now I know, okay?"

"I'm not here about the crackers," he repeated. "I'm here because I want to take you out. Show you around."

"Oh, well, I know the town." Part of me wanted to hug him because he was more big city than anyone else I'd come across since we hit the northern half of this state, but I could barely shake a vampire's hand, so how would a date go?

"Great, then we can skip right past date one and on to date two."

"I..." He was also nearly spit-shined, where most of the guys walking around Shady didn't seem to bother brushing their hair when they woke up in the morning. "Um..." And he smelled familiar, like a department store. "Are you wearing cologne?"

"Yeah, you like that?"

"What's your name?" I asked.

"Jeremy. Jeremy Holmes."

"Okay," I agreed.

"Okay, we're on?"

"Yep. We're on."

"Excellent." He clapped his hands, as if that was one task now complete, and pulled out his phone. "Let me put you in here and we'll plan on Friday."

It struck me as eerily silent as I recited my number, but then he was gone and the noise started back up again.

"You know he's going to drop you in a week, right?" Ethan asked.

"Of course not. How am I supposed to know that?"

Riah dug into his oozing, raw roast beef. I wanted to gag.

"How come I have to toss my crackers," I asked, "but still be exposed to your road kill?"

He pulled a slice out and hung it in my face. I shoved at him and scooted my chair closer to Stella.

"Jeremy wears cologne because he doesn't like half the girls he dates; he's just bored," Stella explained. "But no wolves would date him if they could smell how he really felt."

I glanced at Riah, wondering if cologne would really work. "He doesn't know me yet, so he can't not like me already. Anyway, all I care about right now is that he reminds me of home."

Ethan started: "You said yes to a date—"

"—with the smoothest boy in school—" Stella continued.

"—because he reminds you of home?" Riah finished.

I shrugged. Chicago boys were definitely smoother, on average, in a good way, than Riah or Ethan, but I couldn't very well say that now, could I? I patted myself on my back for the restraint, seeing as I'd stuck my foot in my mouth enough in the past two days.

"*He*, of all people, is the one who reminds you of home?" Riah repeated.

"I can handle it," I assured.

"Oh, we know, Grace James from normal world. You can handle anything."

I didn't like Riah's tone of voice, so I ignored it.

———

It took all day to shake it off, the feeling Riah had left me with. What I'd gathered in the hours after lunch was that Jeremy wasn't only the smoothest boy in school, but also one of the coolest. That wasn't so bad, I decided, as I walked into skills to find Christian waiting for me.

I assumed he was waiting for me because his elbow was propped on his desk, cheek resting in his hand, and he was watching the door from the moment I walked in. Only then he stopped watching the door to follow me as I crossed the room and sat down. Then he had to go and say, "I'm not sure you know what you're getting into."

I heaved out an exasperated, melodramatic sigh. "You too?"

"Jeremy's sort of a purist."

"Ah! The purist nonsense! Please, do tell!"

"Do tell what?"

"What a purist is."

"You don't know what a purist is?" He raised his brow.

With a heavy sigh, I replied, "I really do not."

"Purists think we should live by instinct. Live pure, you know?"

"Like, no more blood bank?"

He nodded. "No more wilderness for the full moon, no more sirens on land, no more trying to keep our thoughts hidden."

"So, why wouldn't Stella want to be the one to tell me that?"

"She probably didn't want to scare you."

"Why would that scare me?"

"If we gave in to instinct, without caring what it might lead to..." The hint of his pause sent shivers down my spine. "Do you have any idea what that might lead to?" he asked.

"A lot of dead people?"

"A lot more than that," he muttered. "Listen, Jeremy's one of my best friends, but he's..."

"Dangerous?"

"No, more like—"

"Then consider me warned."

"You're a novelty, Grace. He'll be bored with you by next week."

I didn't need to tell him off, he saw it on my face.

"That's not what I meant. I mean he *always* gets bored by next week."

"Well, he won't get bored of me." I knew that was just my pride talking, but it felt like all I had left.

The bell saved me from having to discuss it any longer. At one point during Mr. Turner's short lecture, Christian stretched his leg out and pushed the tip of his shoe against my foot, as if to get my attention.

I rolled my eyes to him and sent him the word *obnoxious*, since we were all about calling each other adjectives apparently.

Charming, was his reply, which was accompanied by, I had to hand it to him, a pretty charming smirk. Maybe it was the literal twinkle in his eye that had it coming off that way. Then, *Careful.*

Careful? I echoed, working on the lilt at the end of the word that made it a question. I tried again; it was oddly difficult to get right in my head. Then a third time, working my expression to make it clear it was a question.

Food, he replied, pointing at me.

Well, if I was food, so was he. I jabbed a finger back at him, let it hang across the aisle.

He shook his head and pointed at himself. *Siren.* Then, in a second burst, *con...* Forming something on his lips, he glanced at Mr. Turner. *Contam...* Closing his eyes, he wrinkled his nose and finally spit it out: *contaminated.*

I clapped quietly. "Five syllables might as well be a sentence!" I whispered. He beamed.

"Grace?" Mr. Turner appeared behind me. "That's not how we communicate in this class."

"Of course, I'm sorry. But Christian got out a five-syllable word!"

"Very nice." He nodded. "But keep it up here." Tapping his head, he smiled and shuffled away.

Christian put his hand up for a high five, his smile still huge and genuine, lighting up his face in a way that his ocean-in-the-sunlight eyes couldn't even manage. It only faltered when my palm touched his. I pulled back before he did, and he blinked at me, as if surprised.

Surprised by the contact, which he'd initiated—or surprised that he felt something in it?

Maybe he *had* meant lovely yesterday. Not that it changed anything—he did have a girlfriend—but maybe I wasn't so blind here after all.

It would help things, if I weren't.

Chapter 5

House Marinara

There was one stoplight in Shady Woods.

One.

It was convenient though, being able to pinpoint the center of town, knowing that everything seeped out from there. The movie theater sat at one end of Shady Avenue while the blood bank sat at the other, with one city block of businesses between. The length of one city block anyway, broken up into eight little Shady Woods blocks.

As my mom drove me to Parrino's, where I was meeting Jeremy, though she thought I was meeting Stella, I texted Charlie: **See, can't say I didn't learn anything from you**.

She was around tonight, and I was taking full advantage of that before she disappeared again. She'd gone serious with some boy, and that left her with very little to zero time for me.

I tried to tell myself it would've been the same if I were there. That it wasn't because I'd moved away. That she hadn't actually forgotten me.

So proud! she replied.

The light finally turned green, and my mom pulled through, continuing on Main Street, past Shady Ave. Behind us now was mostly houses and the schools, while the two main streets were lined with all the normal stores, just in case. Everything *looked* normal, of course, even the blood bank. But that didn't mean it was.

Parrino's was Italian, the place we always ordered pizza from, and recently I'd been told it was Ethan's dad's. I guess I could've put that together if I'd tried. Ironic, though, since vampires themselves didn't eat. Plus, the garlic thing. Apparently, they didn't use garlic, but shallots and a "touch of lemon zest" instead. My face clearly expressed what I thought about that, when Ethan had explained, because Riah had gone on and on about how good the food was until I'd wanted to stuff my apple in his mouth.

My mom pulled up to the curb and I got out, waved her off, and walked inside. There was a short staircase that led up to the empty hostess stand, behind which stood a wall that split the restaurant in two. A sculpted, cherry wood bar was to the left, with heavy black curtains covering the massive front windows, and the dining room was to the right. Though it had the same heavy curtains, it was significantly more quaint and romantic. Brighter and whiter.

A staircase led down at the back of the bar, and seemed to be heavily trafficked by the waiters.

Then Mr. Parrino walked up to me.

"Oh, hi, sir." I'd been back in his house once since the day he'd kicked me out and had done my best to avoid him.

He let out a sort of "Mmmm," and I awkwardly went back to texting Charlie.

Scary dad owns the place, but it's cute!

I gave her a minute to answer, but she didn't.

I added, **The restaurant, not scary dad.**

Though really, he was kind of good looking for a dad. Oh, right, vampire. I shook my head, wishing I could text her that. It was bad enough keeping secrets when I lived there, but now they pressed in on all sides and didn't let up.

He's watching me, I told her.

No answer.

If he had a towel hanging over his arm, he'd look like a killer butler. I added.

LOL

I frowned. *LOL* wasn't hard to type; it didn't take anything. How about a conversation here, *Chuck?*

She was named after her dad, who was named after his dad, who was named after his dad. It went way back, to be honest, and when faced with a male-less generation, they went for Charlotte, or Charlemagne, or Charlize.

Charlie had lucked out with Charlotte, but all of them—girls and boys—went by Charlie.

Killer like murderer, not like a good butler, I clarified after rereading my text. **What are you dooooooooing?** I finally asked, exasperated.

My mom had dropped me ten minutes late because I wanted to be sure I wasn't there before Jeremy. Now it had been another ten minutes, and even my best friend was ignoring me.

I looked up at Mr. Parrino. "You don't have a table for Jeremy Holmes ready, do you?"

He shook his head.

"You're not even going to look?"

"You're going to do that again?" he asked.

"Sorry, I just,"—I looked at the time on my phone—"he's late."

Mr. Parrino studied me a minute, during which he may have singed me with his scrutiny. Then he looked down at the papers below him, shuffled a few, and looked back up. "I have no reservations for Jeremy Holmes. And no one is currently seated, waiting for someone."

I know, I know. After what everyone said, I shouldn't be surprised. But wasn't he supposed to reel me in before tossing me back out?

Mr. Parrino rested a hand on the outside edge of the hostess stand. "Don't be sad."

"I'm not sad."

"Too bad. I like you better sad than snarky."

"Fine, I'm sad."

His lip twitched, and I was going to guess it was a smile. "I could find you a table while you wait," he offered.

I looked up at him. "But what if he doesn't show up at all?"

"Then dinner's on the house."

"You won't tell Ethan?" Or Stella, or Riah? That would be so humiliating. *Karma*, my brain corrected. That would be karma, for talking like I didn't care about how long this lasted in the first place.

"Of course not. It's none of my business." He grabbed a menu and motioned his arm out for me to walk with him. "Seating, serving, and cooking for you—that is my business."

He was being so nice, and I'd been such a brat to him. "I'm sorry, Mr. Parrino," I blurted out. "I'm sorry about my dog."

Pausing at a beautiful wood table near the window, he pulled a chair out for me. "Let's forget about your dog." He set the menu in front of me and added, "Also, stay away from the house recipes."

I looked down at them. "Why?" But he was gone.

White candles of different sizes were grouped together in the center of the table, and more silverware than I'd ever seen surrounded my plate. The white napkins were artfully arranged to look like flowers, and my silver goblet was already being filled with fresh water. I'd been to a few high-end restaurants in Chicago in my life, and this ambience did not disappoint.

Nice work, Mr. Parrino.

Pulling aside the drape, I peered out into the dusk-shaded street. There were people closing up the general store kitty-corner across the road and a few cars pulling into the grocer, but no Jeremy walking the sidewalk.

Dropping the curtain closed, I wondered why I did care now, when I hadn't before. I didn't like him like that. He'd just reminded me of home. Home, which was also ignoring me. Okay, so there you go.

I think I just made up with scary dad.

No response, of course.

"Nice earrings," Jeremy said from behind me. He sort of slugged me on the shoulder, then took his seat.

I frowned. "Where've you been?"

"Am I late? I don't really pay too much attention to time."

I stared at him, but it didn't pull an apology.

Instead, he added, "Too bad we couldn't get a table in the cellar, huh?"

"What's the cellar?"

Leaning back in his chair with a smile like he'd just won, he stretched his long arm out to rest it on the table. "I thought you didn't need a tour of town?"

"I don't."

"Sounds like you do."

I rolled my eyes. "Just tell me already?"

"Admit you need a tour first."

"Fine, I need a tour."

He straightened in his seat, now smug. "When they built the town they dug a bunch of tunnels, so we—the vampires—wouldn't have to go out in the sun. No one really uses them anymore, but everyone still loves the cellar."

"Why don't you use them anymore?"

"I guess we got used to it. Or we aren't as pure as we used to be. My grandma's grandma was a siren so it's easier on me than if I were one-hundred-percent vampire. I'm fine if I keep my skin covered, especially with all the shade around here."

Pure? There was that word. Was he referring to genetics, or theology? Not that I wanted to know.

"What does it feel like?" I asked. "The sun, I mean."

"Like you're being pinched all over." He said this with no humor at all, before picking up his menu.

I frowned. That didn't sound pleasant, but it was crazy interesting. Part of why I was drawn to nursing was because of how different vampire, wolf, and siren bodies were to ours. When I was really little, I told my mom I wanted to know about all of them, all of us, inside and out—how we were different and how we were alike. Then I got older and realized human biology was the only biology nursing schools covered.

Jeremy drummed his fingers on the table and looked at me thoughtfully. "Listen, I am sorry I'm late. But most girls your age would wait even longer for a nice meal like this, especially with a guy like me."

I burst out laughing, which caught Mr. Parrino's attention. Maybe because it ruined the ambience, or maybe because he had my back.

Yeah, I think he had my back.

"What's so funny?" Jeremy asked.

"You're assuming I'm new to a nice meal like this."

"Well, you're certainly new to a guy like me." And he winked at the waitress, who arrived at our table in time to witness my epic eye roll.

Jeremy ordered a "tall glass of the cellar's best" and an order of the house marinara. Then he added on a shot of rat blood.

She gave him a look. "Why do you always have to play with fire?"

He put a finger to his mouth and shushed her.

"I'll take the shrimp scampi." Handing her the menu, I folded my hands in front of me on the warm, smooth table, and turned back to Jeremy. "I thought you didn't eat."

"I don't *need* to eat, but tonight is a special occasion."

"*Please.*"

He tilted his head and pulled a candle in front of him. "I shall now punish myself for as many seconds as I was minutes late."

Attention focused on the flame in front of him, he plunged his hand into the fire.

I shot up straight in my seat before remembering he was a vampire and could quite easily heal himself. "That's... unnecessary," I told him.

Vampire or not, the skin started to blister and bubble off his palm. Not *off* off, but blistery drips of skin sunk deeper and deeper into the fire until I was afraid it would spill right around the edges like the wax was doing.

I glanced away, toward the waitress headed our way. "Please stop."

"Not until I've rectified the situation."

"You are not rectifying any situation." But I couldn't not look. It was fascinating because I knew it wasn't permanent. "You're just making me ill."

"Really?" The tone of his voice was the most surprised and unsure I'd heard out of him yet. Flipping his hand to catch the melted strands, he grabbed the shot glass of blood on the waitress' tray. As he dumped the rat blood into his cupped, damaged palm, she set the larger glass down next to him and hustled away.

"What do you mean *really*?" I asked. "Who would find that charming?"

"Grace James, you are seriously no fun."

I stiffened. "Ex*cuse* me?"

The skin on his hand smoothed, then sealed itself healthy.

"I'll have you know I'm plenty of fun."

He wiped the blood off on his napkin, leaving a crimson streak on the stark white linen. Not very cool to stain their stuff like that, to be honest.

"I'm sure," he muttered. "For a normal."

"Says the idiot purist."

His turn to stiffen. "If anything, I'm elitist. Get your facts straight before you attack."

I ran my hands over my face. This was the most awful date of my life. Not that I'd been on many. But I was pretty sure they weren't supposed to be so combative.

I should have left then, but my curiosity got the better of me. "Okay, what's an elitist?"

"You don't really know anything, do you?"

"Thanks, let's just make this worse than it already is."

But my ignorance relaxed him at least. His irritated, straight back fell into a cool, relaxed vampire slump. "An elitist is some-one who thinks abnormals are elite. *Above-normal*, you know? Mainly, I don't think we should be hiding away like we're the problem, when we could be the solution."

I stared at him, at his hair all perfectly settled, eyebrows prob-ably tweezed, nose so straight it could've been formed by a sur-geon. I stared at him because he was a complete idiot, and yet, we *could* be the solution. There were definitely ways we could help the world.

Reaching for my purse while also resting back in my seat, I was considering whether to stay or go when the waitress set a plate in front of me.

Letting out a shriek, I scrambled back in my seat, then cursed myself for acting like such a normal. Where did I think I was? Chicago? Of course the shrimp was served live—for the sirens, *duh*. It shouldn't bother me that their little legs were struggling to escape from the slippery spaghetti underneath. But I couldn't get the thought of shells crunching under my teeth out of my head. And those tiny legs scrambling across my tongue in a last attempt at freedom made me gag, right there at the table.

Jeremy swapped my plate out with his and handed the waitress mine. She looked at me like I was crazy, but took it away.

"Thanks," I muttered, a hand flat on my chest, holding my sanity in.

"No worries. I'm really not that bad, I promise."

I was hungry. After all this, and in spite of it, I really was hungry. So I'd eat quick and then go.

While I ate, he drank out of the tall, thin glass the waitress had brought him earlier, and I marveled at how awful normal was starting to feel. What had been everything to me in Chicago was getting tagged as boring, not fun, and naïve here.

It made me eat faster, so fast I didn't care what it tasted like. Honestly, I didn't know what Riah was talking about. It wasn't all that great—a little on the salty side with a strange undertone that fought the tomato.

When the bill came, Jeremy grabbed for it. Dropping cash on the table, he flashed his fangs at me. I squinted at him, trying to figure out if he meant this like a wink. Gauging it on how proud he seemed of himself, I was going with yes. Proud of himself for paying. I rolled my eyes. Didn't he know pride ruined the effect?

Outside, a cool breeze rushed up to greet us, and Jeremy stayed by my side as I headed down the street.

"I don't want a tour," I told him.

"Well, wanna make out?"

"Are you joking?"

He looked at me. "That's the fun part of a date. I thought that was the part you were talking about, when you said you were fun."

I stopped and stared at him. But what was there to say to that? So with a shake of my head, I started walking again.

At the next intersection, we had to wait for a car to turn. He leaned down, and I thought he was squinting at something on my face, but as I reached a hand up to wipe my cheek, his lips landed on mine.

Surprised, and mortified, I spit in response. Not a real loogie or anything, but spittle. Like if you got a bug in your mouth and were trying to get it out.

"Whoa," he muttered, straightening back up. "Is that how normals do it?"

"No, that's not how normals do it!" Covering my face with my hands, I sputtered, "What? Why?"

He tilted his head. "What, why, what?"

"Our date did not go well. Don't you usually *not* kiss if the date doesn't go well?"

He shrugged. "You're cute."

I groaned and ran a hand through my hair. "Don't ever do that again."

"Fine, fine." He put his hands up in surrender, and I almost, theoretically, wanted to cry. The first kiss of my life and I'd *spit the guy away from me*.

Awesome. This could not get any worse.

"I'm walking you home, though," he said.

"There's no crime in Shady Woods," I said, to let him off the hook.

"My mom would never forgive me if I let a nice girl walk home after dark alone." He grinned. "Not that I'd call you nice."

I pulled my phone out to text Charlie. It would help me ignore him. Then I realized that it *could* get worse, because I couldn't explain to Charlie how many things had gone wrong. Couldn't explain the candle and the rat blood, or the live shrimp, or how I'd almost just had fangs in my mouth.

"Besides," he said, cheerily, "there *is* crime in Shady. Have you heard about the vandals?"

Blinking back tears, I scrolled through the contacts in my phone. Father, mother, brother? That would be a new low. Then my eye caught on Stella Clark.

Well, why not.

That was miserable. And the BEST part was the shrimp scampi I ordered.

She, I would have to tell Charlie, responded right away. **Lol. Did you eat it??**

NO! Jeremy gave me his.

Which was????

The house marinara.

A few minutes passed.

Oh, Grace. But it came from Riah's number.

What happened to Stella?

House = blood.

Then, to top it all off, I doubled over and threw up.

Chapter 6

Need a Hug?

You okay?

    You okay?

    You okay?

From all three of them—Stella, Ethan, and Riah—when the one person who should've been pestering me for news on my date wasn't.

I'd ignored them last night when I'd gotten home, but now I was sitting cross-legged under my comforter, chewing my lip and trying to decide how to respond.

No, I'm not okay. I just want to go home. Where I fit in. Where my best friend won't ignore me. Where I know the rules. Where I'm special.

My thumb lingered on the delete button. No way I would send it, but I was caught, staring at the words.

Was it true?

Had I felt special back there, even though I'd been trying so hard to be normal? All this time had I been proud of what I was destined to become, even while hiding it?

Not that it mattered; a person couldn't be both special and normal. Not at the same time.

My brother's knuckles ran across my door. Zeus responded by wagging his tail, knowing this meant breakfast was ready.

My dad was into Saturday morning family time, and the scent of bacon was wafting up from the kitchen. Shoving my phone in my pajama pants, I crossed the room and let Zeus out to tear down the stairs.

"Morning, kid," my dad said, as he dished waffles onto the plates my brother was setting on the table.

"OJ?" My mom asked from the fridge.

I nodded and sat and yawned. Zeus settled at my side, patient but alert, waiting for anything to drop.

"How was your date last night?" my brother asked, with a smirkety smirk smirk.

I froze, only my eyes moving from him to my mom. "I didn't have a date last night."

My mom set a glass of OJ in front of me. "You know we like it even less when you lie about it, right?"

She was the softie. I snuck a look at my dad. He didn't say anything.

I slumped in my chair. "How'd you know?"

My mom sat down and narrowed her eyes. "I talked to Charlie's mom last night and she mentioned hearing something about it."

"You can't date until you're sixteen," my dad said.

"I can. I'm perfectly capable," I corrected. "I'm just not allowed to."

"Really? Right now you want to get smart?"

"Better than getting stupid," I mumbled.

"I heard that."

Justin pointed a fork at me. "Plus, it's not funny the millionth time you say it."

"I wasn't trying to be funny."

"Hey," my mom scolded. "He's not the one who told on you."

Wrapping my hand tighter around my fork, I took a deep breath and tried to get myself under control.

"What about for the carnival?" I asked, another shot, but this time my tone was level and curious instead of snarky. "Do I get a date for the carnival, or would you rather I kiss some rando during the firework finale?"

"You can kiss your mother," my dad replied, without skipping a beat.

And when nothing else was said about it, I put my fork down. "You're not going to punish me?"

He and my mom shared a look. "We know you're adjusting, and as we're certain it won't happen again, we're going to let it slide. This one time."

"Plus, you got home well before curfew," my mom added.

Justin snickered. "Crappy date, huh?"

"That doesn't even begin to describe it," I admitted, trailing my fork through the syrup on my plate. "Why can't we just go back to Chicago?"

My parents shared another look, though it was much more serious than the first.

"We're not going back to Chicago," my mom finally replied.

"Maybe you need to stop being so obstinate," my dad said. "And start learning the rules."

"What rules? Are you saying the bad date was my fault?"

"How can we know?" my mom asked, with a raised eyebrow. "You won't tell us about it."

"The nicest thing he did was let me eat his food, because I ordered the shrimp scampi. Know what he ordered?"

"You ordered the scampering shrimp?" My mom put a hand over her mouth, trying to stifle—or maybe hide—a laugh.

"What is he?" my brother asked. "Siren? I'd peg you to be into a siren."

"There's only one thing worse than live shrimp," I said. "So it really shouldn't matter what he is."

"Frankly, I gag on raw meat." My mom shook her head and put a hand up, like she was swearing on it. "Give me a shot of blood over raw meat any day."

"Well, raw meat would've ranked higher on my list than live shrimp." I forced a bite of waffle into my mouth, comforted by the fact that it was warm, soft, and without any sort of past life.

"I've got it!" My dad shoved his fork up in the air. "House marinara!"

"Ding, ding, ding, ding."

My brother looked around the table. "What's so wrong with marinara?"

"Thank you!" I cried. "That's what I thought." This game was actually cheering me up a bit.

"It's a vampire-run restaurant," my mom said.

"Where blood can be easily disguised in tomato sauce," my dad added.

Justin's fork tumbled to the plate, and he looked like he might throw up.

I knew how he felt.

There was a knock at the door, and my brother stood to get it. Riah was trailing behind him when he came back into the room.

"Hello James family," he greeted. "I'm Riah Jenkins."

"Yes, Amy's son." My mom smiled. "Would you like a waffle?"

"Sure, I can always stand for more breakfast."

There wasn't another chair at the table, so he sat at the counter and reached for one of the extra waffles my dad had under tinfoil on a plate.

"What's up?" I asked him.

He shrugged. "I was on my way to Ethan's and thought you might want to join us."

"Grace can't date until she's sixteen," my dad told him.

"Gee, thanks, Dad."

"She wouldn't have me anyway," Riah said, tearing into the waffle like it was a cookie. "I'm too hairy for her."

Justin snickered. "Yeah, those sirens better watch out."

I groaned and started shoveling more breakfast into my mouth.

"Grace, you're going to choke," my dad said.

"Good," I mumbled, with my mouth full.

Justin pointed at me. "And that right there, Dad, is why you will never have to worry about her dating."

"I don't know," Riah said, studying me thoughtfully. "Wolves are all about stuffing their faces, to be honest."

One last piece of strawberry, which I made sure to drench in syrup. "I'm grounded, so..." So you can get out of here, is what that meant. Without me.

"No, you're not," my mom said cheerfully.

I looked at her pointedly. "Sure, I am. You just said earlier."

She smiled at Riah. "Grace would love to hang out with you all today. She's been having a real hard time adjusting."

"Okay, well, maybe I don't feel like hanging out today."

"Sure you do," Riah said, in unison with my mom.

"Go get dressed," she said. "We'll keep him company until you're ready."

And that was when I wondered if she was truly diabolical—if *this* was my punishment for lying to them about the date. I would've preferred to be grounded. I would've preferred to wallow.

—ele—

"I need a crash course," I told Riah, once our feet landed on my front porch and the door was shut behind us. "I'm going to try to fit in, but I keep running into things that surprise me."

"Okay, but first, can I give you a hug?"

"Uhhhm...because why?"

"That text you sent this morning. I'm glad you feel you can unload on me, and of course this has been hard on you. If I had to try and live in a normal world, I can't imagine what kind of mess I'd end up in."

My mouth was agape. *That text I'd sent?*

"I'm sorry if I've been hard on you. I didn't really think of what it might be like—I mean, until you told me. You should've just said something earlier, you know?" He ducked his head a little so we were eye to eye. "We're on your side."

I faltered through a bunch of dumb *ums* and *buts*. Then, finally, "So all last week, all that making fun of me, was being on my side?"

"Well, no. That was making fun of the snobby city girl who thought she was too cool for us."

I buried my face in my hands. "I didn't mean to send that." Peeking through my fingers, I asked, "Did it go to all of you?"

"I think just me."

Dropping my hands, I let out a sigh. Better him than all three of them.

"Well, I don't feel so special anymore, but I *am* glad you sent it. It made me realize I've been kind of a jerk."

I stumbled off the steps and started across the lawn to Ethan's.

"Maybe you've been kind of a jerk too, right?" he prodded.

"You need an apology after I just humiliated myself?"

"That's not humiliation! That's vulnerability. That's truth. Humiliation is hairy monster arms." He held one out in front of me with a grin.

"Your hairy monster arms aren't that bad," I admitted. "They're just not quite normal."

"Yet, you still call them hairy monster arms."

"Only because you did." I said with a smile. It faltered when I reached Ethan's front porch, though, and I thought of all I had to learn. But I could do it. I had to.

I had to at least try, because no matter how temporary this was, I couldn't be miserable for the next four years.

Chapter 7

Under the Radar

Another weekend without Charlie, Matty, Rea, or Allie.

I stuffed the ache of losing my normal life down deep and tried to focus on the crash course I'd received. This was my life now, and I was going to master the day-to-day of Shady Woods if it killed me.

Watch, instead of charging ahead, Riah had said. *If you jump in too quick, you end up sounding like an idiot or eating blood spaghetti. Ask one of us, and if we're not around, then assume there's an above-normal option on a menu or an above-normal viewpoint that's different from what you're used to.*

He was talking about dogs, that last part.

Unfortunately, this went south pretty quick: In algebra, second period, a couple sophomores around me burst out laughing, and I asked them what was so funny.

"Jen said something funny is all."

"No, she didn't. She didn't say anything at all."

The girl tapped her head. "We talk up here."

She spun around and walked off, leaving me slightly stunned in the hall. It made sense, I supposed, if you were only friends with dendrites.

Relax, embrace it, had been from Ethan. *Just because it's not what you knew back in Chicago doesn't mean it's bad. Remember, we're the closest thing to superheroes this world has got.*

Then gym happened, where I was paired up with a vampire named Johnny for softball. We were just to toss the ball back and forth to each other, but he had to go and shake my hand—good sportsmanship or something else super polite like that.

Unfortunately, I pretty obviously recoiled. Ethan and Stella swooped in.

"What happened?" she whispered.

"His hand," I whined. I don't know how many times I had to say it, but squishy gave me the shivers.

Ethan shook his head, guided me away, and handed me the mitt he had for Stella. "Take my hand," he instructed.

"What?"

Putting his mitt under his armpit, he grabbed one of my hands with both of his and started squeezing.

I made what I can only assume was an awful face.

"Way to not look down on us," he muttered.

"It's creepy!" I cried. Spongy. It bounced back. I mean, *gross.*

He leaned forward and I heard a click in my ear. I jerked back to see him smiling casually with his fangs.

"I'm going to make sure I have a blood mustache tomorrow morning," he said. "You're going to have to walk all the way to school with me like that, every day until you're used to it." He smiled wide, so I could see his fangs clearly, and I cringed deep inside.

"I'm such a failure."

"Try, try again. Now, let's play catch."

Stella and Johnny were already doing this, and when I glanced over at them, Johnny tossed me a little wave. So no hard feelings, hopefully.

Stella's advice had been:

Above-normals are more traditional. You have to have some respect—like, if they tell you not to bring a dog into their house, you listen, and say "thank you, sir." In fact, maybe you should just be more careful with everyone in general. Like, this thing with you and Christian—Sofia makes people's lives miserable for fun.

Except, then Christian was standing in front of my locker as we came back from gym. Stella shook her head at me but walked past without a word.

I considered nudging him with my hip to get at my locker. It was something I would've done yesterday, but today... Well, I refused to fail at *everything*.

Tomorrow, if I could master the other stuff, I'd worry a little less about pissing off Sofia. But today, I could do this one thing. One. It couldn't be so hard. No matter how amazing his eyes were.

"I tried not to ask about your date in English," he said.

"And you succeeded."

"But I'm not finding it as easy to wait until skills."

"You're not, huh?" Don't worry, I said that carefully, not flirtatiously. Okay, fine. I said it a little of both.

"Do you want him to ask you out again?"

Closing my locker, I leaned sideways against it. "He'd have to be delusional."

"So that's a no?"

Carefully and sincerely, he was staring at me. So, fine, I'd play: "What if I did want him to?"

"Then I'd carry on my way."

"And if I didn't?"

Our faces were maybe eight inches apart, my right foot and his left almost toe to toe. Christian opened his mouth, but before he could answer, Sofia swung into view and placed her hands on her hips, hair somehow looking like it was spiked to a point where it hung down over her shoulder. Before I had a chance to back up, as all my crash course advice came rushing back to me, she slammed her foot between ours, breaking us apart. With one, quick move, she yanked him away, and I stood there as the halls began to clear.

Riah was leaning against his locker. "Not doing too well, are we?" he asked.

I hung my head and started walking. "He started it."

"That's what they all say, before their throats get ripped out."

I snapped to attention. "Sofia's going to rip my throat out?"

He waved it off. "That's more a wolf thing."

"She didn't hear it, but Riah, he pretty much asked me if I liked him."

"And you said?"

"I didn't." We swung into the lunchroom.

"Well, don't."

"What if I do?"

"What was rule number thirteen?"

"Don't ripple the calm sea of Shady Woods."

He slumped into his seat, slapping his brown bag on the table. "You don't want to pick a fight with that girl."

"That seems pretty stupid, that if her boyfriend likes me and wants to break up with her, it's somehow my fault."

"I saw what she just saw, and she's going to blame it on you."

"But I didn't do anything!"

Defeated. That's how I felt.

Defeat wasn't a terribly long walk from despair, and I spent lunch with my head on the table, while my three new friends talked about me as if I wasn't there. They shared all the funny stories of failure I'd managed to gather in just one day and wondered over my head if I actually had it in me to fit in.

How ironic that I couldn't fit in, in the one place I should be able to.

Being normal, inside this world that wasn't, should be easier than being normal in Chicago, where I had to hide so much of myself. Except now it was like I was hiding the other side of me—not my nature, but my personality.

—— *ell* ——

On the way to biology, I ran into Jeremy.

"You haven't told anyone about our date?" I asked.

"What's there to tell?"

"I spit on you. Then I threw up."

"No hard feelings."

"Really?"

"Really." He flashed his fangs at me with a wink, then took his seat. I pulled out my phone to text Ethan that it was almost charming this time, but it got yanked out of my hand.

Sofia, smug, scrolled through it like a mother might. I tried to grab it back, but she held it up and finished whatever she was doing.

Note to self: Put a password on my lock screen.

Tossing it in my lap, she sat down next to me. "I was looking for Christian's number, so you're not dead yet."

I fidgeted, but fixed my attention straight ahead. "If he gives me his number, that's his problem."

"No, honey, that's *your* problem. I will make it your problem."

Under the radar, under the radar, stay under the radar.

"You will have nothing to do with him," she hissed. "Do you understand?"

That is up to Christian.

She narrowed her eyes, as if I'd managed an entire sentence, accidentally, in her head. How does a person zip up their brain when they can barely zip up their lips?

The bell rang, and whether it was by design or not, she made no move to go back to her seat. Instead, she spent the hour staring at my profile, and I spent the hour willing myself to ignore her.

Her perma-sneer was unhinging, and with about ten minutes left, I couldn't take it anymore. I shot my hand up and asked for a pass to the bathroom.

Mr. Reinard had informed us last week that he was not about pee-pee breaks, as he referred to them. Pee-pee breaks were for babies, and as semi-adults we should be able to hold it for the duration of class. Seeing as there was only ten minutes left, I was pretty sure he was going to deny me, but I couldn't stand it one more second. I needed to breathe.

He studied me for a moment, before wordlessly rifling around his desk drawer for the obnoxious sign he'd made to further embarrass those who bothered to ask, but I didn't care. I grabbed it and rushed out of the room.

Out in the empty hall, I didn't really know what to do with myself, since a bathroom was not what I needed. I started making loops around the small school—hall to connecting hall—deter- mined to wait until the last minute to head back in. Then I noticed footsteps behind me. I slowed down and they stopped. I turned but there was no one there.

The echo didn't go away, though, as I headed into the next hallway. I picked up my pace, focused my ears, and decided it was a vampire. The quick pattering was too fast to be anyone else. Turning quickly, I caught only a streak before she was gone, if it was even Sofia in the first place. Except, how would she have gotten past Mr. Reinard? Maybe she owned him, like she owned Christian.

I wanted to spit. Why was I into a guy who was owned in the first place?

Why was I into an abnormal?

Why was I even here?

Chapter 8

It Sucks That Bad

I kept my head down in skills, where we were working on short sentences, and tried to ignore the allure of an even softer side of Christian that showed up when he could tell I was upset.

Melancholic, he'd sent me, drawing out the syllables.

I was melancholic, he was right about that. And I couldn't stand the thought of Stella, Riah, and Ethan talking about me again like they had at lunch, so on the way home, when they turned toward our neighborhood, I went the other way.

"Grace?" Riah asked, while walking backwards.

"I need to clear my head."

"By doing what?"

I shrugged. "Walking."

My phone buzzed: **I wish you were here.**

Finally! Finally Charlie contacted me instead of the other way around. I started heading towards town and called her before she could disappear again.

"Where have you been all weekend?" I asked.

"With the boy." She sighed. "But I hate him now."

"What'd he do?"

"He's being all jealous. He's all 'you can't talk to Matteo any-more.' What an idiot. I mean, don't try to tell me who I can talk to, and don't think I'll choose you over a guy I've been friends with since kindergarten."

I grinned, thinking about them all. "Man, I miss you guys."

"We miss you, too. Hey! How was your date?"

"Right. That. Must really miss me if it took you three days to ask."

"Oh, don't be like that. I was preoccupied. Doesn't mean I don't love you or that I stopped thinking about you. I was just busy."

"I have called you a million times!"

"Yeah, I know, and texted me twenty million."

"Oh! I'm sorry, is that a bother? Wow. Don't let your best friend of your whole life be a bother!" My hand trembled over the button which would end the call. But I couldn't do it, couldn't sever the connection I'd been waiting for all weekend. My eyes filled and I started walking faster, turning right at the intersection toward the blood bank and Al's.

I would walk until I felt better, even if it meant ending up in the middle of nowhere at midnight.

"It sucks that bad?" she asked softly. "I thought, well, I thought you'd be making new friends and stuff."

I chomped down hard on my lower lip to keep from crying as I passed the town's three delinquents, who were out in front of the dentist's office. The wolf was sitting right on top of the tree stump that had been carved to look like a happy tooth, and Legs was making hand motions at me, but not normal people hand motions. They must mean something in the abnormal world though, because they sure felt lewd and they were definitely directed my way.

"It sucks that bad," I admitted. "My date was a total fail, my friends are, well, they're not so bad, actually, but I just want to come home."

"So come home. You can live with me."

Al's Burgers was on the other side of the street from me, and cars were streaming into the parking lot. High school kids, hanging out there after school, similar to what we'd be doing back home. Only, probably not at a place that served who knows what kinds of crazy abnormal concoctions.

Then I passed the blood bank.

I lived in a town with a blood bank. A bank of blood. A brick building with rooms outfitted to take dendrite blood and other rooms outfitted to keep it cool. It even had a drive-thru.

"I wish I could," I admitted.

"You can. Why can't you? Just run away or something."

Charlie had always been the one without common sense. Or, at least, the one who didn't think anything through. Sure, it would make perfect sense for her to run away, make an impulsive decision like that, go where her heart led her.

"It's not that bad," I said. Though, I kept making a mess of things over and over again. Maybe it was that bad.

The laundromat up across the street was the last building in town. It mostly looked neat and tidy except for the charred, blackened corner. I hadn't heard of any arsons on this side of town but couldn't figure what else it would be.

As I reached where the street kept going but the trees closed in, I turned back to survey what I'd be leaving. On the far side of the blood bank, in fuzzy black spray paint, a huge X ran across the side of the building. So, a huge X on the store that kept vampires sane, a charred laundromat, and a smashed light post. It wasn't much.

"Grace?" Charlie asked.

I turned back to the trees and to the road that led out.

"I'm sorry, but I have to go, okay?" she said.

Of course she did. I hung up on her and then I ran.

I'd never understood runners, or track, or any of that. But right then I sort of got it—my feet pounding out the emotion in short bursts, my lungs burning in resistance, burning away the defeat. When I couldn't go anymore, I collapsed on the grass, off the side of the road. One foot to my right was a forest of tall, skinny pines—the vampires of the tree world—and one foot to my left was the road.

The only way in to Shady Woods, and the only way out.

I wasn't sure why I'd picked this, instead of going straight down Main. The beach was in that direction and water was always soothing. Or why I hadn't gone left to the small farm fields that surrounded the movie theater. If I'd wanted to feel deserted, that would have done it.

But I'd chosen the way out. And all that was left in front of me was the back end of the truck stop. The owner was the unofficial gatekeeper of Shady Woods and discouraged strangers from heading toward town. Every time we'd been in there, there'd been no one else, but supposedly he could really talk up the fishing to the north up the highway and the shops further down south.

"Where does that little dirt road go?" people might ask about the one behind the building that led to Shady. And he was said to reply, "To my property and my saw collection. I make axes too, wanna see?" Because they stood for sale in the corner.

Creepy. But that was the point, my dad continually told me.

When I caught my breath, I stood, brushed myself off, and headed around to the front. I could use some water. Maybe a bathroom.

There were three cars in the parking lot, and it was nearly a maze to walk across it, what with all the potholes and chunks of blacktop lying around. The building itself was a mess of a place, with chewed-up wood panels and yellowed windows.

Double glass doors opened onto a little foyer, also dark wood, like it had once been part of the exterior. To the left was a glass door that led into the gas station, in front of me was the one leading to the bathrooms, and to the right was the dingy diner.

I'd never been to the diner part before.

The woman at the hostess stand looked at me but made no move to offer any assistance. I paused for a moment, waiting for her to say hello or seat me, but when she looked back down to her phone, I wound my way past the peeling veneer of the tabletops and the rickety wooden chairs to the back corner.

Tossing my backpack against the wall, I collapsed onto the ripped cushion of one of the booths that ran along the edge of the room. A few down sat two normal guys, or so I assumed because abnormals weren't supposed to come out this far. They didn't look much older than my brother, maybe just out of high school. Probably going fishing. Definitely not headed for the shops.

I folded my arms on the table and buried myself in them. I missed shops—real ones all piled on top of one another.

Footsteps had me straightening back up as one of the guys appeared at my side. "You look like you could use some company," he said from under a beard.

Right out of Wilderness 101, with the flannel and the boots. So maybe that was a regional choice, rather than an abnormal one. "Actually, I could maybe use a ride."

What was I doing? Just because they looked harmless didn't mean I wouldn't get sliced and diced in the back of some conversion van.

Sitting down next to me, he motioned his friend over. "Where you headed?"

"Chicago."

"That's quite a long way."

"Thus the needing a ride."

"This is Rick," he said, as his friend sat down. "I'm Todd."

"Nice to meet you," I said to Rick, who nodded in return before sipping at the water he'd brought with him.

"So." Todd reached an arm up on the booth behind me. "Where'd you come from?"

I scooted over a smidge and wondered if I was thirsty enough to share that glass with Rick. Nah. Where was the waitress, though? Did she do anything around here? "Oh, um..." Shoot. Where had I come from? A secret place you are to know nothing about. "Up north."

"That little fishing village?"

"Of course."

Now he raised an eyebrow. "That's a long walk."

"I can walk a long ways, just not to Chicago."

My phone buzzed. Riah. **You sure you're ok?**

I can't do this. I'm leaving.

I closed my hand over the phone. Was I really leaving? Hitch-hiking wasn't a thing anymore, for good reason.

My phone rang. Riah again. I pushed Todd out of the booth and took a few steps for a little privacy.

"Yes?"

"You can't be serious."

"I'm at the truck stop right now. There are two nice men here who—excuse me! That is not yours!" Todd had reached over to unzip my backpack, but I snatched it away just in time.

Riah snorted. "We'll be there as soon as we can."

He hung up before I could argue, and I sat down in the empty booth behind Todd, next to the one they'd stolen from me.

Reaching out to muss my hair, he said, "Okay, I buy the walking."

I jerked back, further onto the seat, then ran my fingers through my hair. It was long and unruly—not curly but not straight either—and running for miles probably hadn't helped. I'd straightened it every morning in Chicago but hadn't bothered once here.

"You're not supposed to touch strangers like that," I told him.

He shrugged. "We can drive you through Wisconsin, but then you're on your own."

"I'll think about it."

"Well, think fast. We're about ready."

Rick sipped his water, Todd rubbed a twenty between his thumb and forefinger, and I clutched tight to my backpack. There were no spare clothes or snacks in my backpack, but there was an abnormal government text, with its fancy cover and fancy pictures, bookmarked to a photo of the current vampire governing board in the Antarctic. Not that he'd take it for anything—people believed what they believed—but I still felt guilty.

"I think you have to pay up front," I told Todd, when the soft rustle of the bill between his fingers started to agitate me.

"I was giving you time to think."

Or maybe it was the decision that was agitating me. That I wanted to go, but something was holding me back. Sure, common sense, but something else too, when I just wanted to get out of here. I was stalling, even though I knew as soon as Riah showed up, the decision would be made. *Now* was my chance.

I did feel relieved, though, when I spotted them. Riah came in swiftly, with long, determined steps, and yanked my backpack out of my hand.

Stella slid up next to him, then Ethan, with an arm around her waist.

Todd set his lips in a straight line, then said to me, "Friends of yours?"

Riah threw a thumb in his direction. "These guys? For real?"

"Yeah, us guys." Todd stood up and took a step toward Stella. She quickly looked down, away from his stare, to hide the sparkle in her eyes. "You coming or not?" he asked me, as Rick got up and raked a look across Ethan.

"Sorry." I swallowed. "Maybe I'll catch you next time."

As they moved to the hostess stand, Stella slumped into the booth across from me. Ethan joined her and Riah slid in on my side. "We can't leave before they do. They can't know where we came from."

Chapter 9

Siren Tears

"Wait. He drove?" I asked, as Ethan slid into the driver's seat. "He drives?"

"When I have to," he muttered.

Pavement and trees passed in silence, like they were mad at me. It had been quiet at the diner, too.

I squinted at Riah next to me in the back seat, at how hard set his jaw was. "I should've left with them."

He looked over at me in disbelief. "You're not honestly that dumb, are you?"

"Riah!" Stella cried.

He looked to her. "It was careless for her to be there in the first place. Thoughtless. Stupid. Why sugar coat it?"

I rested back against the seat, thinking about how awful it had seemed to Ethan when he'd told me those three 'delinquents' liked to leave town. "I'm sorry. *We've* come and gone, all these years, so I—"

"Your parents never told you how they do it? When they do it? How they stop and ask Jeremy's dad at the truck stop if anyone's been by?"

I swallowed. I'd always used the restroom, or been walking the aisles for a snack, or been preoccupied with the horror of the axe collection.

As we reached the intersection at the center of town, Stella told Ethan to turn right. "Take us to my place."

I scooted closer to the window and set my forehead against the glass as Ethan took the next left onto the gravel road that led to the beach. The way I should've come in the first place.

The carefully manicured trees quickly gave way to untamed overgrowth, and we turned left instead of entering the beach parking lot. I'd never been this way, down this street, and I tried my best to spot the houses through the trees as we passed them. They all sat a bit off shore, and each was different from the next. Some were neat old homes, others simple cubes, and a few loomed larger, new and shiny and modern.

Ethan pulled up in front of one of the older ones, dressed in yellow and trimmed in white. Everyone got out, so I guess that meant I had to, too, and we walked through what was now a drizzle, over a short platform.

Stella stopped both Riah and Ethan before they made it all the way to the porch. "Girls only." She pulled open the screen door and motioned them off. "Go."

We stepped into the living room, which was super outdated. The couch, for example, was one of those tweedy green and yellow things you see in photographs clearly from another time.

Stella moved to the stereo in the corner and turned it on. "Okay, what's up? Like, really?"

I dropped my backpack by the door. "It's like I don't have a home." I expected her to reply, to tell me I hadn't given it enough time, but she didn't. She just flipped to another radio station, then another, but not like she wasn't listening. Like she was waiting for more.

"I can't be myself here, but I could never really be myself there, either. I can't talk to my best friend anymore, because of all the abnormal things I can't say to her, and I can't talk to anyone here without saying something stupid. Plus, my parents aren't even the same. It's like they've been waiting my whole life to be back here, which is a surprise, so maybe they didn't even know it themselves, but either way, they never showed me how to do it right."

"I do understand not feeling at home anywhere," she said, swinging into a little hall and motioning for me to follow.

"Shady doesn't feel like home to you?" I didn't buy that. She'd grown up here.

"Sirens are meant to be in the water—in the ocean. All the time. So your Chicago is my Shady Woods, and your Shady Woods is my Iara."

We entered a nearly empty kitchen, with smaller-than-average appliances, no microwave, and only two chairs at a very small table. Stella settled in front of the sage green cabinets. It took me a minute to sort through what she'd said, and also, "Iara?"

"Lower Shady."

Oh yes. Sure. The lake homes hung above the water because they were connected to a house beneath, in Lower Shady. "But that's just where you sleep."

She shook her head. "My favorite candy shop is down there, and my old school. Some of my childhood friends don't come up for high school, so I hardly see them anymore. I left a life down there just like you did."

"But why do you do it?" If she didn't have to... "Why not stay in Lower Shady?"

"One, because my mom and I don't get along. And two, because my dad thinks it's important to know the land before you explore the ocean."

"So you're just pretending up here? Like I was in Chicago?"

"Pretending? Sure, I guess you could put it that way. Everyone thinks we're so graceful, but really it's that we're tired and worn out—slow—from being dehydrated all the time. Plus, when you're made to move in the resistance of water, this is easy."

I wanted to hug her, so much that tears might have welled up in my eyes. Because she did know what it felt like. Because she could understand me in a way Charlie never could. Because it made a very small part of me, like a big toe's worth, feel like everything might be okay.

She studied me. "Did I just make it worse?"

I shook my head. "Not at all."

"Okay, so let me show you why we're worth protecting then?"

"I never thought you weren't worth protecting. I get all that."

"You might get it," she said, "but you didn't take it seriously today. It's your duty now, living here, whether you like it or not."

She opened a cupboard and I noticed a tear trailing down her face.

"Stella?" I took a few steps toward her. Had I said something? I was always saying something, but so far she'd only been amused, not upset.

Grabbing for a shallow glass bowl, she held it under her chin to catch the silver that had tracked lines down her face. As they came more quickly, she leaned over it.

I blinked a few times. Was I dreaming?

"Um, Stella?" It sounded like tiny pebbles being dropped. I wished I could cry silver tears. They were beautiful. I mean, who can sob and still be entrancing while doing it?

She blinked hard and stood up straight, wiping the silver dust off her cheeks. Taking my hand, she turned it palm up, then scooped a small handful of the silver into it. It moved as one soft, relaxed unit, like how molten metal or cooling lava might, if it weren't so hot and you could handle it. With a sort of pulse, it created its own current, *in my hand*, like I was holding an ocean.

It even sort of smelled like an ocean, like fish and salt and seaweed and tulips.

Okay, so I know the ocean doesn't smell like tulips, but siren tears do.

"Is this going to suck my skin off?" Because it kind of felt like it was sucking my skin off.

She laughed. "There's nothing better than siren tears. They can do anything. Well, and then some, if you mix them with stuff. We like to fancy ourselves potion-makers, you know?" She opened the cupboard wider so I could see into it and stared proudly inside.

It was neatly packed with small jelly jars in every color. Color-coded, actually. The bottom shelf started with the reds and orangey-metallics, while the middle shelf ranged from butter yellow to gold, lime green to pine green. The top shelf held the blues and purples and a few pinks.

I sighed. "They're so pretty."

"The older they are, the further down the rainbow," she explained. "You have to use them quick, like within a half hour, or wait years for them to change color. They're stronger the older they are."

"So what can they do?" I pointed at a shiny coral. "Like what can that one do?"

Stella wrinkled her nose. "I don't actually know. They want us to be older and more responsible before they let us play with the hard stuff. Skills, year three, I think." She plucked a sky blue from

100

the top shelf. "I think this is the one my mom used to change my nose the year I went to the carnival as Pinocchio."

I gaped at her. "You changed your nose?"

"*I* didn't. My mom did. I could make you something with these, though." She glanced at the shallow bowl of fresh silver. It did sort of look like it was waiting for us to do something. Or maybe it was just that it had the same charming effect that sirens did. "A facemask, for example; I'd just need an alligator pear. It'd be like the stuff you can buy in the window, but ten times more effective."

"The window?"

"At the general store." She studied me. "You've never been to the window?"

"What are you talking about?"

"On the side of the general store, there's a window." She stopped as if this would clear it up for me. It didn't. "So you climb through it and there's a roomful of stuff. Abnormal stuff. You've never heard of the window?"

"No. And why a window? Why not a door?"

"To keep normals from finding it. You know, in case someone like you might lead them into town."

I blinked. This had all been a lesson. A lesson in appreciation and duty and friendship. But I still felt better.

My phone started ringing. We both looked toward the living room where it was coming from, then I checked the clock hanging on the wall over the door.

I'd missed dinner and not texted home. My parents were going to kill me.

Chapter 10

Us or Them

They sent my grandpa to pick me up, and as he drove me home in silence, I pressed my finger to the rain that was running down the outside of the car window.

"It was just dinner," I mumbled as we pulled up.

He squeezed my hand. "You're not exactly in trouble."

"Not exactly?"

"They're just worried about you."

"Because of the vandals and the purist nonsense?"

He raised an eyebrow. "You don't keep an eye out and you could easily end up the first in town with teeth in their neck."

I swallowed. "That's an unnecessary picture to paint."

"Is it?"

In the face of his stare, I swung out of the car and ran through the pouring rain to the front door, where Zeus was waiting. My parents too, both of them sitting on the stairs, and I could hear my brother and grandma in the kitchen, chatting over dishes.

My dad's elbows were propped on his thighs, his hands clutched in the open space between them, while my mom was hugging her legs to her, chin resting on her knees.

Both of them relaxed when they saw me but didn't move to stand.

I stood, dripping a little in the hall in front of them. "I'm sorry," I said. "I lost track of time."

"You should've called," my mom said, her eyes dark in the shadow of the enclosed staircase.

"Why didn't you call?" my dad asked.

"I forgot. I'm sorry. I was in a lesson about the miracles that are Shady Woods, I had a terrible day, and I just wasn't thinking about what time it was." Zeus nudged me, as if he'd been worried too, and I let my fingers settle by his ear.

My grandpa came in behind me and sidestepped his way to the kitchen, only to pull a chair out from the table and sit down facing us.

"You weren't upset about that boy again, were you?" my mom asked.

"No. I'm a miserable failure and I wanted to go home."

"We can't go home," my dad said, an edge burned onto his voice.

"Charlie said I could come live with her, and it's like she's almost forgotten about me, so I ran to the truck stop—" I bit my lip. My parents did not need to know about the almost-hitch-hiking. "I don't know what I was thinking; it seemed one step closer or something. I just... I want to go home. Can't we please go home?"

The three of them stared at me, and I noticed, in the severity of the silence, that the water from the kitchen sink had stopped. The chatting over there had stopped, too. They'd all been listening.

Zeus, pressed up against my leg now, was also holding himself still, gauging the room and adapting to it.

"Grace." My mom's tone was laid flat. "We can never go back. *You* can never go back."

Tears sprung to my eyes, and I tried to gulp the desperation back down. My parents were swayed by logic, not drama. "Because of one stupid slip? The girl probably thought she was crazy."

"No," my dad said, dropping his head into his hands and pulling at his hair—the same thick, wavy mop that I had.

But he didn't continue, so I looked to my mom, whose eyes were closed as if she'd hoped this moment would never come. And then, to my grandpa, I asked, "What?"

He cleared his throat before he said it: "There are humans in this world who know about us, and some of them feel it their duty to hunt us down. She was one of those."

"It was us or them," my dad said, to his toes.

I dropped my backpack, which had been hanging in my hand opposite Zeus. "Did you..." Did my dad kill someone because I leaked a thought? Is that what he was saying?

My mom put a hand on his back. "They came to kill us. If we wanted to stay any longer, we would've had to kill every one of them."

"Did you... Is she..." I glanced back and forth between them but my dad was clearly struggling with what he'd done—or what he'd almost had to do. My mom set a forehead on his shoulder and closed her eyes.

My grandma appeared behind my grandpa, with a dish towel and pan in her hands. She was drying, quickly, but the pan no longer had one drop of moisture on it. She kept at it while she explained, "Her cell came for you. Three of them. We thought it best you be gone before they came back to finish the job."

That didn't really answer the question, but I couldn't face the truth of home being suddenly dangerous *and* the fact that my dad had possibly—probably—been forced to killed someone to protect me. So I'd pretend there was a scuffle, my dad had been totally scary and my mom a complete badass, and the cell or whatever ran away.

"Best if you forget about Chicago altogether," my grandpa said. "If you graduate high school and still insist on living normal, I'd suggest picking somewhere else."

My mom glanced up at my grandpa with a frown. "We might be able to visit someday, once you can control yourself. I'm sure they'll have forgotten in a few years."

"Sorry, honey." That was from my grandma, who had finally stilled her hands and was holding onto the pan like it was a steering wheel.

And they *were* sorry; I could see it on every one of their faces. They were sorry I couldn't have what I wanted, even though I'd done it to myself—even though I'd done it to them, too.

That hit like a dart piercing a bull's-eye, my heart being the dartboard.

Spinning on my heels, I launched myself onto the porch before I started bawling in front of everyone. Zeus shot outside past me, and I slammed the door behind us before taking the steps down into the rain.

It had slowed a little and I turned my face up to the sky, closed my eyes, and let the drops wash my tears away. I imagined it was washing this town away, too, and that I was back in Chicago, the cement and brick on top of me instead of all the trees and heavy silence.

Hearing footsteps, I opened my eyes, and with a rush that left me empty, the city slipped away.

Riah walked up to sit on my porch, under the awning where Zeus was sitting patiently, staying dry. "Stella said you might be in trouble, so I came by to see if I could help."

I sat down next to him. "I'm not, really."

"Plus, I felt bad for earlier."

I shrugged. Nothing he could say would hurt me more than I hurt already. It no longer mattered if they laughed at me, or scolded me, or whatever.

"I shouldn't have called you dumb; I was worried. I don't think you know what could happen to you out there."

I wanted to argue that I'd spent a lifetime "out there," but after the conversation I'd just had with my parents, I kept my mouth shut.

"You know, bad people and stuff."

"There are bad people everywhere," I muttered.

"But you're only used to the normal kind."

"Those guys were normal."

"Those guys were creeps, but that's not the point. Wilds prey on hitchhikers, and you wouldn't have been ready for that."

I rolled my eyes to him. "Wild abnormals don't have cars."

He rolled his eyes to mock me, which was somewhat amusing. "At some point, hitchhiking, you would've been walking on the side of the road."

"Are wilds purist?"

"No, they're just trying to get by."

I felt that. I was just trying to get by, too.

Riah drummed his fingertips on the cement between us. "If you ran into a wild on a deserted highway, Grace, they'd see you as nothing but feed."

"But I'm a dendrite."

"Biologically you're human. You just use more of your brain than the rest of them."

"A lot more," I pointed out. "A bazillion times more."

He smirked. "I know. You're so smart. You're the smartest."

I slapped at him, and we both started laughing a little.

What do I smell like? I wondered, when we'd both quieted into the severity of the night again.

He looked over at me, surprise lighting his face. It was the first time I'd spoken to him that way—mind to mind—and I agreed, it felt like we were suddenly closer.

"That was awesome. Do it again."

I smiled. *What do I smell like?*

"Can I smell you? Like, really? Because the rain enhances your non-emotive aroma, so it's hard to say." He turned his nose in my direction and breathed in deep. "From here, all I can tell is it's not one of the simple six."

Yes, you can really smell me.

"You're okay with, like, my nose in your hair?"

I shifted my position a little, braced myself, and nodded.

He watched me for a minute, before slowly leaning in to bury his nose in my hair. Zeus tried to push his way between us, and we laughed again. I shooed him to my other side and held him back. It was oddly comforting, Riah resting against me like that, and me in turn resting into him, shoulder to shoulder, head to head.

It was almost too soothing—folding my strength and making me want to dissolve into tears. A month ago I'd been normal and happy. Now, my dad had maybe killed someone because I branched a word I was supposed to be able to control, and everyone wanted to get at me—purists and wilds and cells of some sort or the other.

I steeled myself. Riah might check up on me every time he thought I was upset or in trouble, and I might talk in his head, soaking up the strength of him next to me, but falling into his lap for a good cry seemed like too much too soon.

"What's taking so long?" I asked, aiming for exasperated to hide the crumble inside. Not that he couldn't smell it.

He pulled away. "Listen, I might not be new to this, but we just started studying the fine details."

"So?"

"So, what?"

"Are you done?"

"No, I thought it was getting too weird for you."

I stared at him for a moment, then set my head on his shoulder. "I'm on to embracing the weird."

His face landed back in my hair and he muttered, "Defeated." Deep breath in. "A little angry." A couple more. "A whole lot lost." Some time went by, but I felt his nose still there, his breath softer, then deeper, then softer. "And some scared. Good. At least you're not in denial anymore."

He straightened, so I reluctantly did too.

"I'd feel a whole lot less lost if I could go home to visit," I told him. "Or if Charlie would answer my texts."

"You can visit me." He knocked his knee into mine. "And I'll answer your texts."

"Wait." I let go of Zeus and he scooted his way between us. "They didn't say she couldn't come here."

"That's a terrible idea. Now you smell like a terrible idea."

"*We've* come here." I jumped to my feet. "Why couldn't she come here?"

"Because you knew our secrets."

"I can't go home, but home could come to me." I hopped past him to the door. "Thanks, Riah. I'll see you tomorrow."

Chapter 11

Small Town Horror Movie

It took a little to convince my parents, but after all, I was the epitome of obstinate. Not to mention, life as I'd known it had been ripped up into irreparable pieces, which was a pretty big bargaining chip, even though normals showing up in Shady was clearly discouraged.

Good for practice, though, is how my dad sold it to the town council, because someone *could*, technically, stumble upon us at any moment.

"It's a little small-town-horror-movie around here," Charlie whispered, as I pushed the cart through the grocery store. "And what's with the furtive glances?"

Those were coming from Nehemiah, the wolf delinquent. I'm sure he could smell how normal she was. He and his friends were standing in front of the dairy case. I swung a left into the cereal aisle as he elbowed Reilly, the vampire contingent of the three. Though I didn't take them for delinquents as seriously as the town did, it seemed smart to get some distance between Normal Blonde Barbie and Death on a Stick.

Riah's dad, who was on the town council, had given us a list of places we couldn't take her. Places that would stick out as weird. The blood bank, for instance—inside was *not* setup as an average blood bank. Outdoors was okay, and the grocery store, because all the weird meats were in a special cooler she'd never think of wandering into. Most of the businesses were set up that way, the abnormal bits hidden just in case.

Anyway, we'd come with my mom to shop for dinner because we jumped at any chance to stock up on sugar.

I was hoping sugar wouldn't just make me more antsy, because come to find out, having your normal friend stay in Shady for a few nights was actually not as great as it seemed. Come to find out, I *did* have a second sense about keeping all the abnormal hidden, which was harder to do here than ever before.

We'd made it home from the airport before dark the night before, so Charlie had missed the conglomeration of insomniac vampires in the square, and we'd taken a long walk after Saturday morning breakfast—with Zeus, of course, because he was sort of a neon sign that announced a normal was around. No one had bothered us, not even my friends. They were to stay away until tonight. Three hours and we'd be in a room full of abnormals, none of whom were used to hiding their weird.

I thought I was going to break out in hives, I was so nervous.

"Why are you walking so fast?" Charlie called from half an aisle behind me. She'd stopped in front of the sugar cereal section.

I knew there to be a few boxes of special Count Choculas about where she was, which, when one poured milk on it, would ooze with dried blood. *A special release for Halloween,* I was to tell her, if she grabbed anything like that. This excuse was also why they'd wanted her to come in October.

Remembering that chocolate cereal was her favorite—Cocoa Puffs, I thought, but still—I hustled back, grabbed her by the elbow, then sped to the end of the aisle only for the cart to smack into Nehemiah as he came around the corner. I let out an "oomph" as my stomach rammed the handlebar. Reilly and Preston appeared behind him on either side.

"You're the new girl," he said.

I gulped. Why was my mom taking so long in the baking aisle?

Charlie elbowed me, and when I still didn't reply, she said, "She is. I'm visiting."

"I can tell," Reilly breathed.

Was he *panting*?

I gave Nehemiah a look. He seemed to be in charge of the other two, so he better help me keep this under wraps.

"What's it like out there?" Preston asked.

"I'm sorry?" Charlie squinted her face up.

"Why don't you ask me on Monday at school," I suggested, finally uncoiling my frozen body into action. I pulled the cart back and tried to go around them. Then again, the last thing I needed was Reilly at Charlie's back.

Crap, was my friend about to be eaten? No. They wouldn't. They couldn't. Everyone had gotten a memo with clearly stated expectations. Only now I wondered if that had sent these fools out looking for her.

Nehemiah moved in front of me again and hushed me, though I hadn't said anything. Unless he was hushing the emotions he could smell rolling off me in a panic. Did bad guys hush you before they killed you?

No. Shady Woods abnormals were *pacifists*.

My nose started to tingle, like right before you cry, and Nehemiah reached a boxy hand out to rest it on my shoulder. "Calm down."

Charlie scoffed. "Do you know these guys?"

I could tell she was irritated and offended that someone would handle me like this, so if I said no, she'd take matters into her own hands. But I had to be the one in charge right now. I had to deal with this. This was my territory, whether she knew it or not.

"Sure I know them," I exaggerated, shrugging him off me. "From school. They're harmless."

Reilly snorted, but it was easily believable of Preston. And I'm not just saying that because he was a dendrite. He really did look like the sorry, naive little brother.

116

Nehemiah's smile curled tight. "Harmless," he repeated.

"What do you want?" I demanded, pushing on the cart, wanting to get through, wondering when and how quickly my mother might find us.

"We're just curious," he said, peering into the mountain of candy in our cart. "We like to wander outside town lines once in awhile."

"Can we please talk about this at school?" I begged.

"Your friends aren't going to let me talk to you at school."

"Why not?"

"They're protecting their find."

"*What* are you talking about?" Charlie asked. "This is the weirdest conversation I've ever had."

Reilly licked his lips. Nehemiah only flicked his attention to her for a moment before returning it to me. "Riah protects his precious things."

"Riah doesn't own me." I shifted uncomfortably. "And I am not a *thing*."

"Like any wolf, Riah would fight to the death for what he considers his own." After a full beat, he pushed off my cart and walked past us. Reilly winked at Charlie as he followed, and Preston mumbled a "so nice to formally meet you," with a little bow. Like I said: harmless.

"Freaking weirdos," Charlie muttered. "Let's find your mom and get out of here."

It took an hour to calm my insides. Then we had another hour before more direct contact. A small party, so she could meet my friends. And hopefully, though there would be more of them, they wouldn't be as obvious as Nehemiah and Reilly. But of *course* they would. I'd be blocking odd comments left and right.

It didn't help that Charlie was pacing the living room. Charlie, and Zeus with her.

"Why are you nervous?" I asked, shoving a handful of candy in my mouth. "You're never nervous. It's making me nervous."

"I'm not nervous, I'm just bored and impatient." She peered out the window. "Are you freaked out by what that blockhead said about Riah? Because to be honest, I kind of am."

"He's an idiot. What does he know about Riah?"

She raised an eyebrow at me. "Probably more than you."

"Aw, are you worried about me?"

She put her hands on her hips. "He'd fight to the death for you? Because he thinks he owns you? Are you sure you're just friends?"

"Of course I'm sure."

"Dude honestly didn't seem to think Riah would let him get near you at school."

"*Dude* is apparently the worst kind of worst that you can find around here."

She mouthed a drawn out, "ohhhh," and I knew she was attaching new labels to them now. Being strung out would explain Reilly, and being the ringleader of whatever would explain Nehemiah. I didn't bother telling her it wasn't like that, because I clearly couldn't tell her what it was like.

"You should meet Rea's new boyfriend. I don't know what she's thinking, but he'd fit right in with those three."

"I wish I could," I muttered.

"You will! For Thanksgiving. You guys have to come back for Thanksgiving, right?"

I shrugged. We'd always spent Thanksgiving with her family, but that would never happen again. Here I thought this trip would make me feel better, but really it just highlighted all the ways I'd changed—all the ways my life had changed—and picked the scab that was never being able to go back.

There was a knock at the door. I jumped up and flung it open.

"Riah!" I cried. "This is Charlie! Charlie! Riah!" And that was as awkward as I'd ever been.

He grinned at me, then at her. "Hi, Charlie." And he held out his hand.

She stared at it, and I felt, suddenly, fiercely protective of him. His sleeves were pushed up to his elbows, showing off all his hairy man hair, and I had to clasp my hands behind my back not to roll them down for him, away from her critical eyes.

Sliding her hand into his, finally, she said, "What is your relationship with my Grace?"

"Um, we're friends?"

"You don't sound so sure about that."

He cleared his throat. "We're friends. You just surprised me."

"Do you think you own her?"

"Excuse me?"

Charlie crossed her arms. "Do you think you own her?"

"Charlie, please," I tugged at her, then quickly filled Riah in: *We ran into Nehemiah at the store... He said you wouldn't let him talk to me at school... Said you would fight to the death for your own, or something like that.*

Riah's face relaxed into a charming smile. "No, I don't think I own her. I'm just not so sure she can take care of herself, which you obviously aren't so sure of either, or you wouldn't be grilling me."

She raised her brow at him, and Riah looked at me. "Do we need to have a talk about this?"

I shrugged. *No.*

"There's more I could explain."

"About what?" Charlie snapped. "More you could explain about thinking you own her?"

He stared at her levelly. "No, about Nehemiah and what he said. He's correct. I would not let him get near her. And if you knew him, you wouldn't either."

I rolled my eyes, but Charlie stiffened. "How do you know he's correct? How do you know what he said about you?"

"Oh." I jumped to attention. "I texted him. I told him about it. Before. In the bathroom."

They both looked at me, dubious.

I shook my head and motioned into the living room. "Can we just forget Nehemiah ever happened?"

"We should talk later, though." Riah said.

Charlie put her hands back on her hips. "That sounds ominous."

Riah rolled his eyes at her and muttered, "Talking sounds ominous? Shows where you're from."

"What's that supposed to mean?"

"Stop it, both of you!" I cried.

They both slumped their shoulders as the doorbell rang. It was Stella and Ethan, and this time my introduction poured out of me in a string of unintelligible syllables. Then I started chewing on my nails.

Stella, in dark brown contacts to hide the silver in her eyes, offered a hand, but it hung there as Charlie sized her up. She was not usually this suspicious of new people. Ethan, always comfortable, stepped between them on his way to the living room and broke the tension. "How was your flight?" he asked.

"Actually, there were these super annoying twins in front of me. Cute, but annoying." She plopped down in the big armchair.

"I hear you," Riah muttered. He sat down and patted for Zeus to join him. "The litter that lives next door is always ringing our doorbell, then running away and laughing."

Charlie's mouth did a weird little twitch. "The *litter*?"

"Quintuplets," I corrected with a choke. "He's just being mean and condescending."

"Quintuplets?" She looked at him. "Didn't Grace say you were a triplet? What are the odds of that?"

Riah looked at me, his face as flat as I'd ever seen it. He was thinking about his answer this time, at least. About how the odds were pretty good here, considering how vampire bodies couldn't support the changes of pregnancy, and how some dendrite scientist figured out a way to extract eggs from his vampire wife in order to create a child with a surrogate mother. How this happened all the time around here, multiple eggs just in case, which often ended up meaning multiple babies too.

"Since when are you so interested in babies?" I asked.

She shrugged. "I'm trying to make conversation."

"Let's start with small talk," I suggested.

"Small talk is lame and boring. Who cares about the weather or what you did yesterday? I want to know the twisted details of a person's life."

Of course she did. I ran my hands over my face.

"Would asking what's for dinner be small talk?" Riah asked.

I stood and headed toward the kitchen, hoping and praying that dinner might save me. You know, what with people stuffing food in their mouths. At the open archway to the front hall I looked back, because none of them had moved. "Food? Anyone?"

Chapter 12

Want Me to Do Something About Jeremy?

After dinner, Charlie insisted on going to the park. It was a warm fall evening and my parents sent us with Zeus and Justin, who swung us by his girlfriend's house on the way there.

Clara was a vampire. Interesting that my brother had no problem with this, when I had such a huge problem with it. They held hands all the time. What about hugs, I wanted to know?

Ethan and Stella promptly took to the sand to snuggle against each other, while Riah, Charlie, and I sat on top of a picnic table, facing the lake. Zeus was on leash, only because it was dark, and Charlie had his lead wrapped around her wrist.

Riah's knee absently tapped into mine a very steady beat, and as Justin and Clara hit the path that brought them into the forest, Charlie sighed. She'd always had a thing for Justin.

"You were hoping tonight would be the night, huh?"

"Why do you think I suggested the park?"

I laughed. Charlie had always liked parks for making out with people. "There's still Riah."

"Wait. What are you offering me up for?" he asked.

Charlie crossed her arms. "You know who I thought I'd get to meet while I was here?"

I rolled my eyes. "He has a girlfriend."

"So? If you put online right now that you were here, I bet he'd show up in minutes."

"He would not."

"Are we talking about Christian?" Riah asked.

I'd spent the last few weeks with my head down and tail between my legs, following the rules. It had been a little spotty even that first week after the truck stop, but I'd gotten it down by now. And since that meant staying away from Christian, at least outside of skills, I obviously couldn't ask him to meet my best friend from back home.

"I dare you," Charlie said. "Plus, if he doesn't show, then he doesn't like you, and you can stop whining about him."

"She whines about him?" Riah's leg stopped moving and he leaned over, resting his arms on his knees. "Really? Grace doesn't strike me as a whiner."

"Do it," Charlie pressed. "I dare you."

"I heard you," I muttered.

She nudged me. "Do it, do it."

With a melodramatic sigh, I pulled my phone out and changed my status: **at the park**—with **Charlie Hall, Riah Jenkins, Stella Clark, and 3 more.**

She nodded, satisfied, and patted my hand.

Then the countdown began.

—*ele*—

I was the first one to see him walk up, with Jeremy of all people. I groaned.

Charlie twisted in her seat. "What? Is he here?"

"Yes. But he's with The Date that will go down in history as Worst Ever."

"Ooh, really? Maybe I can make out with *him*."

"What's wrong with me?" Riah asked, then put his hand out. "No, I don't want to know."

"You're kind of hairy," Charlie and I said at the same time. He shook his head and I laughed, nudging my shoulder to his.

"I'll have you know I'm a mighty fine kisser," he grumbled.

We ignored that, and as Christian and Jeremy reached hearing distance, I swung my feet around to face them. "Hey!" Less awkward greeting: check. "What are you guys doing here?"

Christian raked a hand through his hair. "I saw on—"

Jeremy flicked him and said, "I needed some fresh air."

I couldn't help my smirk. Nope. Not sorry. Charlie stood up with a Cheshire grin on her perfectly made-up face. "I'm Charlie, BFF Extraordinaire. And you are?"

"Christian Riley," he said, offering a hand. "Nice to meet you."

Why they all shook hands, I would never understand. First step to pretending normal, if you asked me, was to never let a normal squeeze a vampire hand. But they did it anyway. All of them. I warned Jeremy in his head, just in case he forgot, *Don't shake her hand.*

"I think this might be the definition of stalking," Riah said. Somehow, though, it came off as jovial.

Charlie glared at him, so I didn't have to. This was what I missed, the kind of thing we did for each other regularly. "Maybe you should come with me," she said, pulling at Riah's arm and dragging him off the table. "Let's take Zeus for a walk, huh?"

"Reconsidering, are we?" Riah teased, as they headed for the beach.

I couldn't hear her response, but at least they'd been getting along better since dinner.

Turning to Christian, I asked, *Why, of all people, did you bring Jeremy?*

He shrugged. *He was with me.*

"Totally rude for you guys to do that in front of me, the secret talky-talky," Jeremy said.

"What if you wouldn't want to hear what I have to say?" I asked him, with a smile.

"I thought we were cool," he said. "And there's no need to worry. I promise to be nice to your human." He put his hand up like he was taking an oath.

I narrowed my eyes, wondering if this was some purist nonsense. "*My* human?"

"You're okay if she wants to make out, right?" he asked.

"Uhhh..." I glanced over to Christian for some help here, but he was trying very hard to look like he wasn't listening. He was staring down at his feet and running the toe of his shoe across some blades of grass.

"I'm crazy intrigued to see if the spitting thing is normal."

"I told you it isn't!"

He winked and headed their way, to where Riah and Charlie were standing by Stella and Ethan. "Who knows!" he called back over his shoulder. "Maybe it is!"

"He's not serious. Please tell me he's not serious." Because Charlie *was* looking for someone to make out with, that had already been determined. She also wasn't very selective who she kissed. Kissing, she liked to say, was one of the few things meant to be spread around. And we were at a park.

"Don't worry. As stupid as he sounds, he's harmless."

"And if not, a little fog never hurt anybody, right?"

Fog: to blur a person's memory, make them forget the terrible thing that happened. Not that I knew how to do that yet; they saved that for skills, year three. But my parents did.

Christian grinned, lopsided. "Completely natural—no side effects, no hangover."

"I don't think I can do this again." Holding my hand up between us, we watched it shake. "Too much stress, having her here, worrying about what she sees."

He grabbed it with both hands and lowered it between us. "I'll distract you."

"Yeah?" I winced at how hopeful that sounded, and he sat down next to me. "What about Sofia?" I asked.

"What about Riah?"

"What do you mean?"

Christian nodded behind me. I turned to find Riah jogging up, Zeus behind him.

"Want me to do something about Jeremy?" he asked.

I frowned. If Charlie handed Zeus off to Riah, she was totally planning on some kissing.

"He just took Charlie into the woods."

I turned to Christian. "I'm sure he'll keep his fangs out of the kissing?"

He shrugged. "We all got the memo."

Enter an ear-piercing, horror-movie scream.

I ran as fast as I could, stumbling over roots and scraping my hands on the brush, out of breath by the time I found them, but it wasn't Jeremy.

Jeremy, if anything, was protecting her, standing between Charlie and three strange vampires. Up close it was clear these wiry stick insects weren't from Shady: messy hair, dirty faces, long traveling cloaks billowing in the breeze. Our vampires were stuffed gluttons in comparison.

Wilds, Christian verified in my head. But Riah hadn't said anything about them ever coming here. They were as scarce as normals in this town, because there were no normals to feed on.

Until now.

"Is she okay?" I rushed to Charlie's side, and Riah rushed to mine. Zeus pulled on the leash, growling at the vampires cloaked in front of us, but I hissed at him to stop and he sat with a whimper.

"She's fine," Jeremy said, not looking at me, not moving much at all really. Clara and Ethan stepped up next to him, the wilds in front of them and the rest of us behind. "We just saw something she couldn't handle seeing."

Her eyes were wide and she was shaking, tears streaming down her cheeks while her hands fluttered like limp birds at her sides. Justin put his hands to Charlie's face, forcing her to look at him. He closed his eyes and began to mutter, but no way was he good enough at all this yet to actually fog someone, was he?

"What did you see?" I asked. Those wilds looked straight out of a horror movie, but that wouldn't explain total and utter shock, would it?

Jeremy motioned off the path, where two men lay. Men and blood. Men *in* blood? Stella rushed over to them. One was crumpled and bleeding. The other looked knocked out.

She saw them feeding? I asked Jeremy.

He nodded, still focused on the three in front of him, still barely moving.

Stella cupped a palm around the bloody guy's neck, and I could see the blood pulsing through her fingers from here. Then the silver started dripping down her cheeks.

Justin pulled back from where he'd been attached to Charlie. "We need to get her home," he muttered. "I can't finish this."

Charlie was clinging to him now, her face buried in his neck, but she seemed more confused now than freaking out. Her hands were no longer fluttering and her breathing had slowed, so he must have accomplished something.

"We didn't realize this was anyone's territory," one of the wilds said.

I went to charge through Jeremy and Ethan and give these three a piece of my mind, but Riah caught me by the wrist. "Look at them for one second," he hissed. "Then tell me that's a good idea."

Zeus let out a whimper.

I blamed the fading light for making them look scary, though, for throwing shadows on their faces and cutting craters into the hollows of their cheeks. Then I saw the one with blood dripping off his exposed fangs, down his chin, and along his neck.

"I claim this feed," Jeremy said, his voice strong.

Feed?

"We apologize. Again, we didn't realize this was claimed territory." The same one who spoke before bowed his head. "We mean no harm."

"What's your business here?" Riah asked, his voice sounding as official as Jeremy's.

"We are but traveling through."

Another guy, but not the one dripping of blood, put a finger up as if he was counting us. "Vampire, wolf, dendrite, siren." Pointing at Charlie, he stopped.

The bloody guy curled his lip back and held his mouth open so no one could miss the fangs... The power... The threat.

Okay, so now I could see the charming in Jeremy's version.

My stomach rolled and a groan caught my attention off the path. Hopefully that meant Stella was having some success.

Christian crouched down next to her. "Should I call my dad?"

Why your dad? I asked.

He's the doctor.

"No, I think I got the wound sealed up." Stella stood. Faint silver streaks shone on her cheeks and a powdery film spattered

131

the collar of the guy's flannel shirt. Then it hit me—these were the guys I was going to hitch a ride with, Todd and Rick.

"Where'd these guys come from?" I asked the wilds. Riah squeezed my wrist, and *ow,* but if he could speak to them, why couldn't I?

"We tracked them from the truck stop."

"Should I call *my* dad?" Jeremy asked, with a note of surprise.

I threw my hands up. *Who's* his *dad?*

He owns the truck stop.

The first wild took another step toward us. "I'm Samuel, it's a pleasure to make your acquaintance. We truly do apologize. We were simply out hunting."

"I'll take them back to my dad," Jeremy said. "I just need a car." He looked at Justin. Justin looked at me and Charlie.

"I got them," Riah promised, letting go of my wrist finally, which I nursed.

"I'll call Dad for a ride home," I told my brother.

Christian put a hand on my arm. "I'm gonna go with Jeremy, in case they end up needing a doctor."

I nodded. His hand trailed off my sleeve slowly, as he moved to join Jeremy, Justin, and Clara.

Riah steered Charlie around on the path and we left first, Ethan and Stella following behind.

"Who are they?" Charlie asked, glancing back at the wilds.

"They're not supposed to be here," Riah muttered.

Chapter 13

Hand of Humanity

Our first order of business the next day was getting Charlie back to the airport safely. Then we made a pact to never bring another normal into Shady Woods, ever again.

It had been a harrowing weekend and my parents were none too pleased that she'd seen what she'd seen and had to be fogged. My mom did not approve of messing with brains uninvited, even when necessary. Though, she agreed it had been necessary.

"We should swing by the Jenkins'," my mom suggested, as we hit the intersection back in Shady. "See what they think about the whole thing."

"What's there to think?" I wondered. A couple wilds had been out hunting and followed some stupid normals through the woods.

"Well, what were those two normals here for?" my mom asked, making me wonder if it had been me they were after. If maybe they were a little creepier than I'd thought. "And why would they have walked into the woods on foot?"

"Hunting?" my dad asked.

My mom looked at him. "Think they're Hand?"

"What do you mean, hand?" I asked.

"The Hand of Humanity." My mom twisted in her seat. "The girl who was after you, that's what they call themselves."

"You mean... I might have brought them here?"

"No. They don't really communicate like that. Locally maybe, but otherwise they're off the grid—small vigilante groups."

That's not exactly what I meant, but I wasn't going to say it. I swallowed hard and slumped in my seat, lowering my gaze to the bruise on my wrist. Thanks to Riah's hold on me the night before, it was pretty nasty looking. "Isn't it hunting season? Couldn't they have been out looking for deer?"

"True, true," my mom said. "Good point."

"And there were only two of them?"

I nodded, catching my dad's eye in the rearview.

"That would be a particularly small cell." My parents looked at each other, then my dad turned back to the road.

"So they *weren't* Hand?" I asked, scooting up again.

"Probably not," my mom said, but not in a very reassuring tone.

"I'd still like to know what the council is doing about the wilds, though."

So that's how we ended up at Riah's on a Sunday night.

We ran through the rain and huddled under the overhang on the porch until Riah's mom opened the door. Their whole family was sitting in the living room, like we'd interrupted something.

My mom noticed this too. "I'm sorry, we should've called."

"No, no, it's okay." Mrs. Jenkin's motioned us in, and we did our best to shake ourselves off on the front tile.

"Why don't you kids go find something to do," Mr. Jenkins suggested. Riah's sisters responded like slingshots up the stairs, and I followed Riah up after them.

I stood in the doorway of his room and studied it for a minute. There was one poster of a football guy I didn't recognize, two of bands I did, one of a wolf, and three smaller pictures of trees and caves and waterfalls. A few dusty trophies sat on his desk, no doubt from ages ago, and an inflatable pink flamingo, which came to my waist, was guarding the door. I blame the flamingo for me slamming my toe into the foot of his bed.

"Ow! *Dang!*"

"Here, let me get that for you." He leaned over to place his fingers under the frame, then stood, lifting the bed up with him. After moving it out of the way, he lowered it back to the floor.

"Speaking of your super-human strength, you know you can't handle a dendrite the same way you can handle wolves and vampires, right?" I didn't know about sirens, but I knew wolves and vampires were sturdier than me.

"What are you talking about?"

I waved my wrist at him. He furrowed his brow and came over to inspect it, then looked up at me like I'd punched him in the throat. "I did that?"

I felt it—his sorrow and self-hatred—deep in my chest. And I knew it. I held my own. "It's fine, really."

But he only shook his head and stood up, walking to the open window where the rain was slashing in. "It's not all right."

"Now that you know you can hurt me, I know you won't do it again."

He set his forehead against the window frame. I stood up and went over to him. Except, "You know water is getting in here, right?" I was essentially standing in a puddle. At least his floor was tile.

"It helps to be outside."

Helps what?

"Helps everything."

The breeze brushed past him and across my face. "I'm not scared of you; I just thought you should know."

No response.

"Really, you're kind of a teddy bear."

He snorted. "I eat teddy bears for breakfast." He said it like he'd been aiming for a joke, but his voice broke.

"What's that look like?" I teased. "Is it fuzzy? You got some in your fridge?"

Now he looked at me, and hard. "I mean I hunt them and eat them, on the full moon."

There'd been a full moon, of course, a couple of them since I'd arrived. He left for the night with his dad and sister, then came back and we never said a word about it.

I blinked. "For real? You hunt bears?"

He responded with a serious crease in his forehead. Then he closed his eyes and tightened his muscles. All of them. Jaw, forehead, fists. "When I'm hunting, Grace, I'm no better than those wilds. I would've made the same mistake as them."

I sat in that a moment, the reality of his above-normal, and decided I should be thankful I was a dendrite. Really, what had I been complaining about all this time? If I wanted a normal life, I could have one. I could choose.

"There's no one better to help me then," I finally said.

"Help you what?"

"Learn how to take care of myself."

"If only that would protect you."

"Riah, you have to stop fighting my battles for me. You don't own me." Yeah, we hadn't really had time to talk about that either.

"I don't think I own you, if anything I think you own—" He gulped the last word down, but I knew what it was.

If anything, he thought I owned him.

Awkward.

"Since you sent me that text, Grace, I've felt responsible for you."

He moved a little and the rain was blowing more directly onto me now. I went to sit on the rug and settled against his bed.

"Of course I'll help you learn to protect yourself, but until you can actually fight those wilds and have a chance at winning, I'll do what I have to do to keep you safe. I can't help it, okay? That's who I am." He came over to sit next to me.

"Tell me they're so skinny because they drink as little as possible so they don't have to kill people."

"They're not so skinny. Shady vampires are so fat because they drink more than they need—enough to make sure their hunting instincts don't kick in."

I raised an eyebrow. Fat? They were literally string beans. All veins and tendons, it seemed, but no real muscle. I started chewing on my scraggliest fingernail. *Tell me what I'm feeling.*

I detected a ghost of a smile from him, and after a long minute, he buried his face in my hair.

My parents found us like that, before he could sort through my feelings, which would have been helpful. My dad's frown had me distracted though, worried as I followed them to the car. Come to find out it was just about me being in a boy's bedroom.

"Never again, Grace. That was an oversight because we were preoccupied."

I rolled my eyes. "I'm more worried about why you were pre-occupied than all of the nothing that will ever happen in Riah's bedroom."

"It's fine." My mom turned in her seat. "Mr. Holmes told the council that the two young men have been traveling back and forth to fish for some time now. He thinks the wilds lured them into the forest to feed, but you interrupted things."

"And what about the wilds?"

"The council is keeping an eye on them to make sure they don't hang around."

"So life carries on as we know it?" I asked.

They didn't reply, but maybe that was simply because they realized life as I'd known it was a far cry from all this.

"Okay, then how about telling me why wolves feel like they own people, or why they feel like other people own them."

"It's the Were Code. Their version of the dendrite's System of Silence."

The System of Silence boiled down to not telling others what we could do with our heads. If you screwed up and they heard you: deny, deny, deny. Deny until they thought they were crazy.

"Now that you know about fogging and placing thoughts, the System takes on a little more meaning, don't you think?" My mom loved to be obscure. When I didn't reply, she continued. "It also refers to the use of fogging, to silence others when absolutely necessary. *And* it refers to placing thought—that we shouldn't. We should be silent *ourselves* in that respect."

"Can we get back to the Were Code?"

My dad raised his right hand in a fist. "I vow to be true. I vow to stand with my pack. I vow to be loyal to the moon."

"What's 'loyal to the moon' supposed to mean?" I asked. "It sounds like a sick go-ahead to kill people."

"It means a lot of things," my mom said. "It means they kill only when the moon tells them, it reminds them to respect life, and it also poses as a symbol. The moon holds power over them and stands for others who hold power over them: their alpha, their boss, their parents, friends, spouses... You get the idea. It means they're to be loyal to those who deserve their loyalty. Above all else, they're to be faithful and true. They're taught to think of what's best for the pack before thinking of what's best for themselves." My mom seemed an endless fountain of knowledge. How had she contained that all those years, pretending to be normal?

"So if someone twisted the code, it could mean they'd fight to the death for you?"

"Even not twisted, there are situations where it could mean that."

I chomped on my lip as it all came together. That kind of devotion—innocuous or not—made me uncomfortable. I was about to ask her if that kind of thing was normal in an abnormal world, but her cell rang.

It was my grandpa, informing her that his pines, the ones that had been set on fire last month, had been set on fire again the night before. The fire had spread this time, scorching a jagged chunk of his field.

Thank goodness it had started raining, he said, or it would have reached town in no time.

Chapter 14

What Did I Miss?

Three policemen marched in during lunch, straight to Nehemiah, Reilly, and Preston. It was the first time I'd ever seen anyone get arrested.

"Is this because of my grandpa's field?" I asked Ethan, seeing as he had the closest ties to the cops.

But it was Riah who nodded through a huge bite of raw meat sandwich. Funny how I'd gotten used to that.

Also funny how Nehemiah, Reilly, and Preston seemed shocked, like they hadn't done anything worth getting arrested for. Funny how they didn't seem to know what the cops were talking about.

"What if it was the wilds?" I asked, after they'd been escorted out.

"It happened before they were around."

"Who knows how long they've been around? Plus, they're much faster than Nehemiah and Preston, and remember, I saw the whole trio at the grocery store?"

"I'm sure the timing works out," Ethan said.

Riah agreed, "It makes the most sense."

"It doesn't, though." They only stared at me, as if this sort of creative policing was acceptable.

"At least they won't cancel the carnival now," Stella offered brightly.

"They would never," Ethan said.

Riah swallowed whatever chunk of meat he'd been working on. "They were thinking about it."

"Maybe they should." I tossed a carrot stick back into its bag, no longer hungry. "Because it's more likely those wilds, and they could still be around. If there's a threat to the town, what better time than when everyone is in one place?" Because I'd heard that too, that every business shut down for the carnival, so no one had to miss it.

"Tonight," Riah muttered.

"What?"

"Tonight would be a better time. When all the wolves are gone for the full moon." He shifted in his seat. "Listen, I've been thinking, we should go to the carnival together."

I looked at him. Then tried not to look at him. Carnival dates kissed each other during the firework finale. This much I knew.

He cleared his throat. "I mean, as friends, for your protection, you know? The four of us."

Still awkward. But I nodded. "Um, sure?"

With an appeasing smile, he elbowed me gently. "There's an inspiring way to say yes to a date."

"A date?"

"Joke. That was a joke."

Yes. Most definitely awkward.

"Don't worry," Ethan broke in, *thank goodness.* "We all know who you want to kiss."

I gave him a look, but at least the question that hung in the air had dissipated: *What kind of moon was I exactly?*

Still, I stood, shoving the remnants of my cold lunch into my brown bag. "I need to, um, run to the bathroom before class."

Winding through the tables, I dumped all my food in the garbage by the hall.

"You all right?" Christian's voice rang out from behind me.

I spun around. "Not really."

"I figured after the park... I wanted to message you yesterday, but... Wanna talk about it?"

"No. I can only talk to you in class." But thank you for reminding me of all the things I had to be upset about, instead of just the strange arrest that didn't make sense and whatever weird relationship I'd walked into with Riah.

"What?"

"I can only talk to you in class," I repeated. "So I don't piss Sofia off. That's how I'm supposed to function here, afraid of everyone and toeing the line." And yet one more thing I'd almost forgotten about, for me to be upset with. He watched me for a minute, and I put my hands on my hips with a huff. "Being afraid and toeing the line isn't easy—it's not me—and it makes me very much not okay."

"So, if there was no Sofia?"

"That would be great," I admitted. "That would be super great."

Taking a few steps toward me, he said, "If there was no Sofia, I would've said yes that first day."

I blinked. That first day, when I'd asked him out. What was he saying? "But there is, Christian. So please don't do this." Don't give me another reason, on top of everything else.

I didn't have time to think about a boy anyway. Or any of the rest of it. I had to figure out who to tell about Nehemiah, Reilly, and Preston being at the grocery store. A teacher? Wait till I was home and ask my parents? Go straight to the police?

With a shake of my head, I turned and headed toward the office, where I ended up spending my Spanish hour. First I told the secretary, who sent me to the vice principal, who sent me to my parents. My mom sent me to my dad, who said he'd talk to Riah's dad, and if the police wanted to talk to me, they would bring me in after school.

I was kind of stunned about it, that no one seemed to really think it mattered that they were at the grocery store, in the center of town, when the fire was started, so I wasn't paying attention when Sofia slammed into me in biology, causing my books to tumble out of my arms.

As I knelt down to collect them, she sat in my seat and crossed her legs.

I'd never seen her look so angry. I mean, I thought she always looked angry, but her expression felt real close to lighting me on fire.

"Think you can waltz in here and steal my carnival date, just like that?" She snapped her fingers on *that*.

I raised my brow. "I have never waltzed once in my entire life." Also, as far as I knew, Riah wasn't her carnival date.

"I will be at your back every step you take, and I will cut you down every chance I get." She leaned over, which wasn't exactly on top of me, but somehow she was able to loom in a way that felt like it. I picked up my stack of books and scooted back, which had me ending up on my butt—embarrassing—but at least out from under her. I scrambled up.

"Do you understand?" she asked, with a tilt to her words like I was an idiot.

I swallowed, determined everyone in class wouldn't remember me on my butt in front of her. Enter sarcasm: "I understand that you'll be at my back every step I take and will cut me down at every chance you get. Looking forward to it." Then I marched over to sit in her seat, rather than waiting for her to get up out of mine.

This was the desk between Jeremy and Aster, one of her best friends. Jeremy snorted and Aster looked surprised—though almost impressed. So I'd take that.

"What did I miss?" I asked Jeremy, as the bell rang.

"Christian broke up with her."

—eee—

Our skills class had moved to the auditorium so we could work on communicating at longer distances. Christian was waiting outside for me, and pushed open the doors as I approached.

"Thanks a lot, by the way," I muttered, as Sofia's words rang in my head. *Cut you down every chance I get.*

He squinted at me. "I can't tell if you're being serious or sarcastic."

"Yes, that's a thing us normals like to do."

The bell rang and we split up to hide in opposite corners of the dark room, the goal to have no visual for where our thoughts were headed. We were supposed to think of the person or picture their face in our mind.

We chatted about nothing for a while, since sometimes messages could get crossed. I occasionally heard a voice in my head that wasn't Christian's and was certain not all of my thoughts were hitting him either. After about twenty minutes, it seemed we were in sync and no longer having any difficulties, so our real conversation started.

You must be serious, right?

You mean, you think I'm thanking you, a lot, for breaking up with your girlfriend?

Well, that makes more sense than anything else.

She just about attacked me in biology.

Ah. So it was sarcastic.

He didn't say anything else, and I sighed. *I'm sorry.*

For what?

Well, isn't that what someone says about a breakup? And I'm sorry I had an attitude about it. It's just, I think she wants to cut me.

She won't cut you.

I made a face, even though he couldn't see it. *It's noted that you didn't argue how she wants to.*

She's kind of angry, as a baseline, he admitted. *You can't think too much about it.* A short pause, then, *I couldn't ask you to the carnival if I had a girlfriend.*

Wait, you didn't tell her that, did you?

Of course not.

So she'd just known. Or guessed. *Did you tell her you liked me?*

No, but I'm not very good at hiding my feelings.

I sat in that a minute. He did always make me feel special, like I was the only one he was paying attention to. Charlie had a way of doing that too, so I hadn't thought much about it, but maybe it meant more from him.

Grace?

Yeah?

Thought I lost you for a second.

You didn't lose me.

Look, I wanted to do it better than this, some big prom-posal type thing, but I suppose that wouldn't be very cool right after a breakup like that, so...

Then I thought maybe I lost him. Could you lose someone mid-sentence? I didn't think it worked that way. Once the stream was there it didn't usually shoot off path.

Christian?

Yeah, I'm here. Sorry. Grace, would you be my date for the carnival?

Yes. It meant more than just a date, too. Like when he said prom-posal, that's how big a thing this stupid holiday seemed to be around here. It was like being asked to come home and meet his family for the first time on Christmas and spend New Year's together, knowing there was a kiss at the end, knowing New Year's was the start of something new. *Oh, but shoot.*

Oh, but shoot?

I told Riah I'd go with him. But I'm sure he won't mind, I mean, he was just being protective and stuff. It was just as friends.

That's baloney, you know that, right? You don't need protection, particularly at the carnival when the entire town will be there to protect you.

I didn't reply. I didn't want to think about it. Sofia had already ruined the asking; now Riah was ruining the accepting.

So... then I'm too late? he asked. *You're going with Riah?*

Of course not. Because I most certainly wasn't kissing Riah at the end of the night. *I'll meet you there, okay? He can bring me, I'll point out how safe I'll be once I get there, and done. It'll be our night.*

I can work with that, as long as you dress up with me.

What?

The costumes? Usually you dress up with your date.

I groaned. I was pretty happy with the prospect of bonfires and candy. Well, and now fireworks and kisses. Did we have to confuse the event with all this other stuff?

I heard that, he said, his voice amused.

Fine, but you have to pick what we're dressing up as.

Chapter 15

Wilds Don't Confess

Like Riah had suggested at lunch, the night the wolves were gone was a prime time to attack.

A quiet, stealthy attack. On the blood bank. Burned to the ground.

I couldn't wait to tell Riah I was right. Because Nchemiah, Reilly, and Preston were being held at the police station, and this time it positively couldn't have been them.

The newspaper spun it as an attack on Shady Woods, that whoever committed the arson was hoping to ruin our peace. Without the blood, those "who needed blood" would have to "go elsewhere" for it.

Reading the Shady Wood Times was like deciphering a riddle, veiled as it was for those in the surrounding communities who might come across it. As I sat at the kitchen table with my mom, looking out the window at the Parrino's house next door, I wondered how long those who needed it could last on what was in their fridge.

And what they would do when it was gone.

"Don't worry," my mom said. "The turnaround on blood is only twenty-four hours."

I looked over at her face, which was actually quite calm and relaxed under the circumstances. My dad had rushed out of the house in an altogether different state only a half an hour before. Able-bodied men were being called to meet at the police station. Some were needed to fight the fire, some were making calls to ensure everyone in town heard the news—including the wolves who were waking from their longest night of the month—and many more were scouring the area and hunting for the wilds.

School was canceled while the search was on, and once it ended—they were found at a camp that seemed fairly well used—we were all encouraged to make our way to the high school gym to give blood and make up for what had been lost.

I was listening to the talk around me as I watched my blood drain directly into a half-gallon container. They hid it much better at the blood bank, where, instead of filling a fourth of this container, I'd be filling up a much less assuming pint-sized bag. There, I wouldn't have to watch it be dumped in with other blood and passed off to a vampire family because there was nowhere else to store it but in their refrigerator.

"Hey." Riah appeared in front of me, his forehead creased.

"Hey! You just get back?"

"Yeah." He eyed the nearly empty container and pulled up a chair. "I wanted to make sure you were okay."

"Why wouldn't I be okay?" I grinned. "I was right, wasn't I?"

He rolled his eyes. "Yeah, yeah. Nehemiah, Reilly, and Preston are students of the year."

"Now that I think about it though, I'm not sure the wilds make total sense either. Take the vandalism, for instance. Maybe the graffiti was Nehemiah."

"Why would Nehemiah put up hateful graffiti about himself?"

"At the grocery store he told me they liked to get out. Maybe he wants to be normal as much as I did."

He raised an eyebrow. "As much as you did?"

"Stop it and listen to me. I'm clearly the brains here."

"You're never going to let this go, are you?"

"Could they really have been around that long? The wilds? I mean, the vandalism started before we even moved in, and aren't wilds all about roaming and not staying in one place too long? Plus, there's no town near here for them to feed off, so no way, had they been here that long, would they have let go of Rick so easily. They would've been starving."

"Are you done?" he asked with a soft smile.

"What's going to happen to them?"

"The council is contacting the Elders. Hopefully they'll send the Vamguard to take them to the Isle."

I cocked my head. "I don't think we've gotten that far in civics."

"What part?"

"Both parts."

"That was three parts." He smirked a little, and I made a face at him.

"The Vamguard and the Isle."

"The Vamguard protects the Elders and vampires in general, and they take care of things if a vampire gets out of line. The Isle is an island where those who refuse to get back in line end up."

"They put their criminals on an island paradise?"

"Where they can only hunt and drink from animals, which means it keeps them alive but never satisfies their thirst."

"Have they confessed?" I asked. Because if they were going to be tortured for the rest of their lives, there should be no doubt of their guilt.

"Wilds don't confess."

I rolled my eyes. More creative policing, and when it had worked out so well for them last time. "What about wild wolves? Would they confess?"

"That would depend on who's asking."

"Meaning, they'd confess to their moon but never against?"

"Metaphorically speaking."

"Right." I kicked my feet back and forth, under my chair. "Riah, I've been meaning to ask you something."

The creases in his forehead reappeared. "Okay?"

But asking him exactly what I was to him, only to turn around and tell him I was going to the carnival with Christian wasn't fair. And it would only make things more awkward. If he felt the same as I did, then the fact that I asked would be weird, and if he didn't, if he felt more... I valued him as a friend—a best friend, even—and I didn't want to ruin that.

"Christian asked me to the carnival."

He managed to convey nothing with his expression. "There's no question there."

"Oh! Right. So I know you were worried about my safety and everything—"

"Especially if the villains are still lurking?" he teased, and I was thankful he was him—the type to make it light and easy on me, even if at my expense.

"They really could be."

He smiled a little. "Where's this question come in?"

"I was thinking you could make sure I get there safely, and then I'd meet up with Christian. Since once we're there, the whole town is there, and the whole town can take care of a few wilds, or whoever it is we're actually dealing with."

"Sure, Grace. Of course."

But I couldn't tell how he mean it. If he was really sure, or if it made him sad. Then I remembered he could smell me and probably knew how nervous I was this whole time. For all I knew, he could smell that I didn't want him to like me like that, so what else would he say?

Ugh, having a wolf best friend was a pain. Or easier than anything else, depending on how you looked at it.

"Hey, Christian," he said, looking past me.

"Hey!" I cried, my voice almost cracking. Man, this abnormal world had groomed me from fairly cool to completely odd *so* fast.

Christian was smiling, probably at my idiocy, and handed me a cookie and a cup of juice. "I heard you needed to be detached." He nodded to the IV and needle in my arm.

"But you're not going to detach me."

"Sure am." He sat down on the stool, scooted closer to me, and pulled out a roll of tape, cotton balls, and some little pads from his pocket.

"Wait."

He grinned but didn't look at me, intent instead on the rubber gloves he was putting on.

"Riah." I looked to him, but he was gone. "Anyone? A little help here, please?"

"I told you he was jealous."

"He's not jealous." I rolled my eyes. "He just knows when to make himself scarce." He knows how much I like you, I didn't add, and he's a good friend and not going to ruin anything. "Or," I added, "he's as scared as I am regarding what's about to happen here."

Christian snickered a little and glanced at me. We were close enough I could see every bit of silver shining from his irises. That and his eyelashes. Plus a freckle above his lip.

"I work at the blood bank in the summers. You'll survive."

"Hey, that reminds me, you said your dad's the doctor?" Chattering was how I dealt with needles. I might want to sign up to poke people with them, but I didn't like them going in or coming out of me. "Is he everyone's doctor or just the dendrites?"

The little pad was damp as he used it to ease the tape up, and that was impressive. I'd meant to close my eyes or look away but now I had to watch.

"Everyone's." Tape was gone, painless—I was taking notes—and he held the cotton ball to the entry point, slipped the needle out, popped it with one hand in the sharps bucket between my chair and the next, then ripped a piece of tape off with his teeth.

Now I was watching him. "Do you want to go into biomedical too?"

"That's a really odd way of saying it."

"Sorry, that's what they called it when we did career planning in eighth grade."

"Probably. I'll either intern with my dad or maybe at the blood bank."

"I want to be a nurse."

"Why not a doctor?"

"Because doctor's don't get to spend quite as much time with the patients. In hospitals, anyway. I want to be a hospital nurse, not a clinic nurse. So your dad learned all the species' biologies? Where'd he go to school for that?"

"He went to med school, then interned with the last doctor here to learn the abnormal stuff. Now eat your cookie."

I studied it. It had raisins in it. And chocolate. Who thought that was a good idea? "*You* eat my cookie."

He snatched it from me. "Then drink your juice. You just gave two pints, and I'm not supposed to let you go until you've had some sugar."

I tilted my head at him as he took a big bite. "Do you really like that?"

"I just decided what we're dressing up as, for the carnival."

Chapter 16

Do Not Look Back

It was the night of the carnival. My first date with Christian. Our first kiss.

I was delaying, due to nerves, and trying to figure out if they were because of how my last kiss had gone or because I hadn't been to the park since the night with Charlie. Riah, Stella, Ethan, and I were hanging out in front of Al's at one of his cement patio tables. We'd had dinner before he shut down and headed to the carnival, along with everyone else.

I imagined them all huddled around the bonfires in wigs, throwing candy at each other like at a parade. Christian waiting for me. Sofia ready to wring my neck.

There was that too. Maybe I was nervous about facing her. Until now, Christian and I hadn't really been anything more than what we were before they broke up, but after tonight, I'd be committing to her wrath as much as anything else.

Adjusting the stethoscope around my neck that Christian had snagged from his dad's office, I stood. "If we don't leave now, we'll miss the sunset." I couldn't keep them forever, and I didn't want to miss too much.

"Does that mean you're ready?" Riah asked, swinging his legs around the bench. He was dressed as a siren, in that Stella's mom had done something to make his eyes sparkle.

Ethan's costume consisted of a scarf around his neck, which he'd wound around both him and Stella. Probably so she wouldn't wrap her feather boa around him. They detangled themselves, and as Stella stretched, the bells on Al's door jingled.

Riah and I shared a look, and I ran through my memory, seeing again how Al had locked the front door, had even yanked on the handle to make sure it was fastened. We spun around at the same time to find three men with gasoline containers stepping out of the restaurant. Two of them I recognized from the truck stop—and from that night at the park.

Todd crossed his arms, his jug clearly empty, while the third guy sloshed some gas from a full jug onto the front door. Rick had the matches and looked from us to Todd.

Todd nodded.

Every sound that followed reverberated in my head, as if my ears were struggling to perceive what was happening, or trying to kick-start my brain into believing it wasn't a nightmare: the striking of a match being lit, the whoosh of a newly started fire, the scratch of Rick itching his chin with the barrel of a gun.

My mind jumbled.

The barrel of a gun.

But he was here because of us, because of Stella. She'd *saved* him.

There were five of them now, and we were surrounded. A few had come up behind us from the street. Riah seemed to be searching for an out, Stella's jaw was nearly unhinged in shock, and Ethan looked ever so slightly disturbed. But that was saying something.

It was amazing how tension could rise without anyone saying or doing anything.

"Rick and I'll bring them down to the corner, figure something out." Todd nodded to the others. "You stick to the plan."

Rick grabbed for Stella and Ethan, and Todd ripped Riah and I apart. I looked back to find that Al's was the third building they'd gotten too, as the laundromat and the bowling alley down the block were growing brighter too. *Snap, crackle, pop.*

Why couldn't I think? Or at least, why couldn't I think helpful thoughts?

Todd was squeezing my arm so tight that in my previous, normal life I might've thought he would snap it right off. Yet now I knew a wolf was the only one who'd truly be able to do that. At least the wolf was on my side. Though he didn't have the gun.

We were shoved all the way to the bank on the corner, where they threw us up against the brick.

"What are we going to do about the vampire?" Rick asked Todd, and Todd motioned them to step away so we couldn't hear them.

The fire eating the buildings seemed audible from where we were down the street. Pieces of charred somethings wafted near us, fluttered to the pavement, and nestled to rest in the gutter.

I thought for one second of my first date and my first kiss. Christian knew I was with Riah. Did he think I was picking Riah over him right now?

Columns of smoke were reaching to the sky, and I wondered how long it would take before someone noticed the smell. Would they be able to tell the difference between the bonfires at the beach and the burning buildings? Would they be so focused on a stupid carnival they waited all year for that they wouldn't notice their town being burnt to the ground?

What are we going to do with the vampire, they'd asked, because the rest of us were easy enough to destroy with a gun.

I began to shake. Riah eyed me, as I'm sure the tremors were reaching him where our bodies touched, and he wrapped his arms around me.

"They must be Hand," I whispered.

Todd pierced me with a glare, "You talking about us? Or thinking you can get away?"

"What do you want?" Stella asked, in an oddly silky tone. Sirens were magnetic to begin with, but that was most definitely some intentional charm.

"If I told you, I'd have to kill you." He waved his hand and laughed, as if it was no matter, as if we were good as dead already. Then I saw him stagger. The charm must have hit him, because he now looked confused and opened his mouth to answer her question. "As long you exist, humans are at risk."

"And what are you doing?" she asked, her voice a little clearer and stronger now.

"We couldn't get the wildfire to spread, so we're burning each building by hand. When you scatter, we'll be waiting to hunt you down one by one."

He shook his head as if to clear it, and I saw Stella drop a little in Ethan's arms. I could feel her charm rushing back to her in a way I hadn't felt it leave. Rick snorted.

Todd clenched his jaw and turned to Rick. "The siren is mine."

Rick waved his gun in the air. "This isn't going to do anything to that vampire."

Glancing back at us, Todd motioned Rick even further away. Should've come prepared, I wanted to tell them. Instead, I turned to Riah.

Are they really going to kill us?

"I can smell it." Riah choked this out on a whisper, as if it was suffocating him.

Hate is one thing, but we're talking about murder.

"They smell like hate and determination and righteousness." He kept his voice low, but it was as certain as I'd ever heard it.

"They think they're doing the right thing, and they have the determination to follow it through."

"There's five of them," I whispered. "There's always been five, not two."

"That's how they burned your grandpa's field, while they were also getting attacked."

Then they did it all. They've been around since the truck stop, probably before that. "We have to do something."

"What in the world can we do?" Stella hissed.

"Run for the beach," Ethan said. "I can buy enough time for Grace to get close enough to call for help."

"No!" Stella clutched his scarf so hard her knuckles faded to white.

"I'm the only one who can take the bullets," he insisted. "I can get you a head start."

Riah nodded. "I'll stay, too."

"No, you won't," Ethan said. "You they could kill."

"Maybe, but the longer we keep them, the closer Grace can get to the beach."

"Maybe?" I squealed. He would so willingly give himself up for what? I choked on my own spit. In all my imaginings, this was not how I saw it go down. I saw him killing someone for me, not sacrificing himself.

"Right," Ethan said, his eyes on me but his words for Riah. "So you should go with the girls in case these guys get past me. A second line of defense."

I was almost put off by this, as if it were a sexist thing, but on second thought, realized it was a species thing. Ethan was mostly invincible, along with quick, and Riah was strong as a bear. Stella could charm people, but that took time and energy we didn't have right now, and I, it seemed at the moment, hadn't learned crap.

"Okay," Riah agreed, turning back to me. "How close do you think you'll need to be to reach anyone?"

"I've never done further than across the auditorium." And that was exhausting enough. "Maybe a few blocks?"

"If we're going to do this, no matter what happens behind you, you need to keep going. You have to focus. You have to get close enough. It's as simple as that."

"He's right, Grace," Stella said softly, reaching for my hand. "The only thing that matters is getting you within range of that beach."

I thought of that night at her house, of her saying it was my duty now to protect them, but it didn't feel much like protecting them if I were leaving them behind to get slaughtered simply because I was our best bet to call for help.

My eyes brimmed with tears at the thought of hearing my friends screaming behind me. Maybe they couldn't hurt Ethan—maybe he would heal. But Stella? How could I run from her knowing she was as vulnerable as me?

"You think you're any match for them?" Ethan asked. "The only way we can win here is to get you to that beach. You need to run and not look back."

I blinked back tears and swallowed the sob that threatened to escape, then nodded hard.

"Say it," Stella demanded.

Okay.

"Say it!" she seethed.

"I promise," I whimpered.

An explosion sounded from down the street, and as Todd and Rick turned toward the sound, Ethan nodded his head.

This was our moment. Ethan took a few solid steps forward, and the three of us slipped around the side of the bank, breaking into a run under the drive-thru.

Don't look back, I told myself. Do not look back.

The angry cries of the normals reached us, and we flew down Main Street, my stethoscope bouncing along my chest. As we reached the grocery store, Stella was starting to lag behind. I forced myself not to hesitate, not to turn back and check on her.

I could hear her, though, and that helped. I could hear each of us as our feet hit the pavement. The wind whipped through my hair as I focused on this steady rhythm, which lasted until we turned at The Bluegill's Perch.

That was where Stella's footsteps stopped and her screams began.

Chapter 17

Only Pain Was Left

I couldn't help it, I looked back.

The building was in the way, though, so I couldn't see anything.

Uncertain I could go on, no matter what I'd promised, I slowed to a stop. Riah had been a touch ahead of me the whole time, as if he wanted to drag me at a faster pace. Now, he retraced his steps, grabbed my hand, and did just that. When he seemed satisfied I was focused again, he let go and headed back for Stella.

The instant my connection to him was severed, a sob boiled up from my chest.

I caught it there, though, and struggled to get hold of myself, because I knew that if I stopped—if he thought I needed him—he'd come for me and leave her.

Only, were his footsteps getter louder now instead of softer? Or was that someone who'd gotten past him?

Our time was running out, and I couldn't keep up much longer at the pace I was going. The trees were getting thicker, but I was still four or five blocks away.

Maybe that would be close enough. It had to be.

I concentrated, gathered, focused, and pushed, using all the fear in every cell of my body as the driving force behind it. I pictured my dad, my mom, my brother, my teachers, my friends' parents. I pictured the crowd as I imagined them at the beach, in the hope it might just hit someone, anyone.

The town is burning! Hand of Humanity! Over and over and over, every step counted. I would run until someone stopped me. *Help! Fire! Hand!*

Riah flew past me then, catching my arm to drag me faster. But before I could even tell him there was no way, before I even had time to stumble, which I would have, no doubt, a hand caught my hair, whipping my head back and causing my feet to fly out from under me. I lost hold of Riah and landed hard on my tailbone. The pain seared through my body, taking over my consciousness and washing the fear and panic away.

Only pain was left.

Sour breath rested on my face as Rick squatted over me. Using his leverage on my hair, he twisted my cheek into the dirt road beneath us. "It's a nice night to save the—"

Riah knocked him over, off me and onto the shoulder of the road. His fist dragged me a few inches before it loosened its hold on my hair, and I tried to get up, wanting to help, to do something, to fight, but I found it nearly impossible to move. My breath was just starting to come back to me, and the pain in my lower back was blinding. I could see Rick's gun lying a few feet from me on the road, and I tried to get up.

Even if I could reach it, though, would I be able to use it?

He shoved Riah into a tree, but in a second Riah was back and they were circling each other. Riah took a hit, and another, again and again. I could barely stand to watch but couldn't force myself to turn away—I felt like if I did, I'd be abandoning him.

I struggled onto my knees. Riah was obviously not an experienced fighter and was taking far too many hits, but that didn't seem to be bothering him. He seemed more puzzled than anything, as if he was trying to figure something out.

Then he finally landed a punch. It hit with such ferocity it even sounded different than Rick's. Though the noise of the fight had started to fade in the background, the impact of that particular hit was so startling, I jumped. It sent Rick flying a few yards, his arms wind-milling to reclaim balance with no success. Landing on his butt, he managed to find his feet just as Riah approached with another.

This second hit of Riah's was even more severe. He seemed confident and sure of himself now, and he threw his body behind it, launching Rick with such force that the tree that stopped him shook to its very tips. He let out a moan and slumped to the ground. Riah glanced over at me, but before he could take a step in my direction, Rick was pulling himself to his feet and lurching toward him again.

The pain in my back was down to a piercing throb, and as I tried to stand, I heard another set of feet coming from town.

Todd. What did that mean?

I grabbed the gun, not sure what I was going to do with it, but at least it was something.

Then there were more feet, a deafening patter coming from the other direction. I looked toward the beach, and the sob, now one of relief, burst out of me.

The adult vampires were coming so fast they were almost a blur, so fast I could feel the air churning as they approached.

I let the gun fall out of my fingers and covered my face with my hands, no longer able to stop the fear and panic from rushing back in and consuming me. Riah scrambled to my side as the Shady vampires slowed around us. I clung to him, and he clung to me—clung around me, really, as Rick and Todd realized how outnumbered they were.

Good luck, I thought, as they ran and the air whipped past us again, our vampires in pursuit.

Ethan's dad and Riah's mom were the only ones left once the crowd cleared. Also, somehow, my dad. He checked me over but I assured him I was okay.

Stella!! I wailed in my head as loud as I could. *Ethan!!*

"Right here," Ethan panted.

I gasped in relief as he came into sight, limping and pulling Stella behind him. She ran to me and we threw our arms around each other.

"How many are there?" my dad asked. "I need to tell them what they're hunting for."

"Five." Ethan went into a quick description of each, and my dad ran a few yards up to send the message.

"Are you okay?" I asked Stella, clinging to her now, and feeling like I'd never stop clinging to one of them for the rest of my life.

"Yes, you?"

I nodded.

"He only had time to lick my face before Ethan stopped him, said he wanted to know if I tasted like fish." I could feel her tremble before she pulled back.

"I'm so sorry, Grace," Ethan said. "I couldn't keep them both for very long. The big guy got away almost immediately, and when I heard Stella scream, I had to follow. It left the other one to come after you."

"It doesn't matter," I told him. "We did it."

"Are you limping?" his dad asked.

"He got shot," Stella answered. "Only once, somehow. He'll be okay."

At this, Mr. Parrino pulled up Ethan's shirt. I stared in wonder at the hole near his hip.

Ethan gritted his teeth as his dad messed with it, spreading and poking it with his fingers. Thick vampire blood leached slowly from the wound. It would have poured out of the rest of us, but on him it leaked like an oversaturated sponge. Thick, dark, and gelatinous.

I managed to hold in my shiver.

Mr. Parrino dropped Ethan's shirt and shot into the woods. Ethan's face twitched as he tried to hide the pain, and Stella ran her hand up and down his back.

Riah was answering the questions his mom and my dad were throwing at us, but once Mr. Parrino reappeared I was only paying attention to him. He held a limp raccoon in one hand, its neck hanging as if it had been snapped, and shot me an apologetic look. I gulped as he tore the fur off its neck with his fangs and lifted Ethan's shirt to let the animal bleed on his wound. Ethan sighed almost immediately in relief.

"Now drink it," his dad instructed.

Ethan made a face. "I'd rather heal on my own."

"I'm not having you ooze out for a week before this heals up. Drink."

Ethan huffed but took the raccoon and lowered his head to its neck. It wasn't the vision, but the soft sucking, like a baby on a bottle, that made me look away.

An engine idled nearby, and I lifted my head to find my dad's truck. My grandpa was driving and my mom flew out of the cab before it was parked. Justin, my grandma, and Riah's dad hopped out of the back, along with Ethan's stepmom, who was dressed as a vampire with plastic fangs in her mouth, and an abnormally gorgeous couple in fancy ball attire.

I'm fine, Mom, I told her, before she even reached me. When she did, her fingers danced along my arms and face, checking over every inch of me. I leaned into her, to stop it, and because I needed her arms around me.

The woman with long white hair rushed to Stella and clutched her to her chest. "Baby!" she cried. "Are you all right? Do you need my tears? I can fix you; I'll fix you."

Stella shrugged her off, backing up into the man I assumed was her dad. His red wavy hair stood out as much as her mom's white mane. "I'm fine."

Ethan's stepmom gave him a hug, and Riah's dad (who was wearing a bear head as a wig) joined his mom (wearing a wolf head—but the animal kind and not the werewolf kind, I assumed) in thumbing over Riah's injuries. His face was pretty messed up, and I noticed, though his parents didn't, that he was holding his shirt at his waist, as if he knew he had bruises forming there too and didn't want them to worry.

Mr. Jenkins checked over Riah's knuckles, then let go. "All in a full moon, eh?"

Riah's glance skittered over to me and then back, but he didn't reply, as if he didn't want me to think about what he did on a full moon. I hadn't held it against him before, and frankly, I didn't care at all anymore. The good in Riah outweighed the however

175

many hours a month he didn't have control over himself, that was for sure.

As his mom reached for his hand, the one lingering on the hem of his shirt, I charged him for a hug. If he didn't want her to see, it was the least I could do.

"Thank you," I whispered. "You were amazing. I mean, hands down, the best." I let go. "The best friend, the best everything. Also, can you teach me how to do that?"

"I wish," he muttered. "Then you wouldn't be such a thorn in my side all the time." Before I had a chance to take him seriously, not that I would've, he grabbed my hand. "I didn't mean that. I don't know why I'm joking right now. I wasn't sure we were going to come out of that, and I need you to know, Grace..." He cleared his throat. "As best friends go, you're my favorite."

As best friends go. Maybe he was like Jupiter, and had a bunch of moons. Maybe we were on the same page.

"You seem oddly calm about all this," my brother announced, taking me from Riah and forcing me into a hug. The tweed suit his girlfriend had talked him into was scratchy, and his monocle dug into my cheek. Their friend group had gone to the carnival as Clue characters, and all these costumes around me made the entire night feel oddly surreal. Like a play.

"It doesn't feel real," I admitted, touching the stethoscope still hanging from my neck. "But I'll probably wake up in shock tomorrow morning and not be able to speak."

He snickered. "That would be a huge improvement."

I smacked him, and he smacked me back, and my mom got her stern voice out. "Really? Even now, you two have to do this?"

My brother winked at her, then pulled me into another hug. "That was pretty cool, Grace, scary as it was. Everyone heard you. It felt like we were all connected when you spoke at us like that, some hive mind or something."

Mr. Jacobson, dressed as a mountain climber, came running from the direction of town and called for my dad. "Tell everyone we have them, all five. They didn't even split up, just went for their car. We need the council."

"Oh, thank *goodness,*" Stella's mom cried, dabbing at the silver streaks on her face. This only made them more noticeable though, because she was really just spreading them around instead of wiping them off.

My mom looked at her funny, then shook her head. "That was fast."

"Yeah, I don't know who they thought they were messing with." Ethan's dad clapped him on the shoulder. "Let's get you home for some rest, huh?"

Chapter 18

We Are So Leaving

"Grace?" My mom knocked on my door late the next morning. "Christian's here, honey."

I shot up, then groaned. Oh, but I was sore. And my *tailbone*. Plus, I was pretty sure I looked like a horror movie, considering I came home the night before and went straight to bed. After all that adrenaline wore off, there wasn't much choice.

"Can you keep him busy while I shower?" I asked.

"Of course, honey."

It was just what I needed. I turned the temperature up and rotated under the hot water, so it could ease all my sore muscles. I was sleepy, and the warmth seemed to soothe that too. I could have stood there for an hour, or as long as it took before my mom yelled at me for wasting all the hot water, but Christian was downstairs.

He had to know that I hadn't stood him up. I'd meant to text him last night, just in case, but everyone was buzzing around us and then when we got home, I literally crashed.

When I finally swung into the kitchen, he was on a stool, looking ten times fresher than I did. The sight of him was especially potent, and I stood there staring at him until my mom interrupted me with a hug.

"Ow."

She held me at arm's length and studied my face. "Do you need to see Dr. Riley?"

"No, I'm just sore." And there was a bruise on my tailbone the size of a small plate, but I didn't think I needed a doctor for that.

She kissed the top of my head and left the room, so I moved over to the counter and sat down gingerly on the stool next to Christian.

"I'm sorry I didn't show," I said at the same time that he said, "Are you really okay?"

I nodded.

"I heard you last night—everyone did—and the panic in your voice... They said you were okay, but I couldn't sleep. They told us we had to stay at the beach, or I would've tried to come see you, and then when they let us go, you were gone. I just... I had to make sure, for myself, that you were in one piece."

"I am, and I didn't mean to stand you up."

"Clearly."

I tilted my head a little. "Are you being sarcastic? Because I can't exactly tell."

He smiled. "Yeah, that's a thing us abnormals do sometimes."

I grinned and relaxed. This was okay. We were okay.

He poked my knee with his finger. "You missed your first carnival."

I rolled my eyes.

"So you wouldn't want to go the park with me, then? Because—" He looked down at his shoes and began to kick them against my stool. The vibration radiated pain through my tailbone, but I was going to keep that to myself. "I thought we could try this date thing again. Go do the candy hunt with the kids, since you never got to do that before either."

I waited for him to look up at me, then replied, "I'd love to. But first, I feel like I owe you a kiss."

He laughed a little. "Well, I wouldn't want you to feel obligated."

I swallowed and channeled some bold Charlie. "I'm not waiting for the next fireworks."

"No? Because I could probably find some in our garage."

If I kissed him, maybe the nerves would go away, the way my fingers were tingling. Tapping them against each other, I stood up off the stool and considered stepping between his legs. But then he stood up, so okay. He put a hand to my waist, then moved it to my arm, and I was over the awkwardness of it. Stretching up

181

to meet him, I placed my lips to his, softly—no spitting. Then he kissed me, and I kissed him, and he kissed me, and it was the most sweet and the most perfect.

We pulled away at the same time, too, also perfect, and I kept my eyes closed for a second, to rest in the feeling of my stomach melting straight through.

When I opened them, I realized my hand had found his shoulder. My hand on the front of his shoulder, his hand on my arm. But we just stood there, staring at each other.

Until my dad's footsteps pounded down the stairs.

I shot backwards, clambering against the stool. Christian caught it and righted it for me.

"Come here, Grace," my dad said from the archway. I walked over, and without so much as a glance in Christian's direction, he said, "I heard there's a boy here."

Christian jumped up and came toward us, hand outstretched. "Hi, Mr. James, I'm Christian. It's nice to meet you."

My dad did not take it.

Dad, be nice.

But Christian dropped his arm back to his side and moved on. "I was hoping to take Grace to the park today, so she can experience a little of the carnival, if that's okay with you."

"That sounds like a date," my dad said, crossing his arms.

"Of course, sir, I wouldn't want to take her out without your approval." Christian met his eye, politely and without squirming. "Maybe if we went with some friends? Or if you'd prefer, we could just hang around here."

Wow. I took a step back to better watch them.

"Do you like my daughter?"

Oy. I bit my tongue and curtailed my brain power, successfully for once.

"I do, sir. Very much."

"No dates."

"No dates," Christian agreed. "Of course, sir."

My dad let out a small, amused laugh, but hid it behind a cough. "You don't need to call me sir."

"Sorry, Mr. James."

"I don't want to hear about her having a boyfriend until she's sixteen. And no dating until then either."

I opened my mouth to object, but my dad's look shut me up so I settled for hands on my face to cover my surely red cheeks.

"Of course, Mr. James." Christian nodded firmly. "You won't hear about it. And no dating."

My dad raised an eyebrow. I squirmed. "Where's your mother?" he asked.

"Right here." She stepped in and raised her hand with a small smile. "For the record, I don't mind hearing about it."

"We are so leaving now." I grabbed Christian's hand, dropping it as soon as my dad cleared his throat, and led him out the front door.

Chapter 19

Cut and Dry

Six months later and I still had one problem: Sofia.

Christian and I started off slow the first few months, and then after spring break he joined me at our lunch table, making it official as far as the rest of school was concerned.

Since then it had been two months of avoiding her, lest she 'cut me down'. For instance, as I was packing my bag on the last day of school, someone shoved me hard from behind.

My head would've slammed into the edge of the locker door and probably split open, if Riah hadn't stepped over to yank it out of my way. "I smelled her coming," he explained.

She was walking backwards, away from me, and her face lit up with a satisfied evil when our eyes met. Only once she was sucked into the crowd did I lean back against the metal and relax.

"Is he worth it?" Riah asked, while messing with the locker door that he'd pulled too far open and now didn't seem to want to go back.

"I thought so."

He snorted, giving up with the tinkering and trying a quick shove. And then it was swinging again, how it was supposed to. "But now you're starting to wonder?"

"Now I'm starting to wonder what I'm in for."

We both watched Christian approach and I elbowed Riah, not wanting him to tell my now-boyfriend what just happened. He shrugged, then went back to finish up in his locker.

"Everyone's going to Al's after school," Christian said. "To celebrate."

Al's was finally rebuilt, after having to wait for the blood bank to be finished first. It was going to be a zoo, though, and I'd oddly come to prefer the sparseness that this small town offered.

"We were thinking of going to the beach," I told him. And since the park was sort of our place, where we had our first date, along with our second and third kiss... I smiled. "Please?"

A newer problem, related to Sofia, was that all his friends were her friends. We hadn't really spent any time with them yet, and I wasn't sure how long that could go on before he got sick of it.

This very well might be the moment he'd pick his people over me, but he twined his fingers through mine. "Of course."

"With my friends?"

"Sure."

"Not with yours."

"Yeah, I get it."

"Because it might be a little soon for that."

He nodded.

"I mean, it might always be a little soon for that."

He frowned.

"We'll worry about it later."

Riah cleared his throat from a few feet away. Stella and Ethan were there too, waiting for us.

I pulled my phone out to text Charlie: **Happy last day of school!! <3 <3 <3**

I knew she wouldn't reply for another hour, based on when she got out of school, or maybe not even for a day, based on our friendship difference, but I was still attached to her—to all of them—and that wasn't such an easy thing to let go of.

She wasn't such an easy thing to let go of.

As we walked to the beach, I mulled over being normal again, what I'd thought it meant and what it meant to me now. I'd spent my life identifying with them, wanting to be them so badly it had burned shame into my psyche.

I guess I should've known it wasn't that cut and dry. If the world of normals wasn't that cut and dry, why would the world between normals and above-normals be any more so? Evil could be found anywhere, and left unchecked it could take the most innocent of us down. It had nothing to do with who we started as but everything to do with the choices we made and the person we intended to be.

The Hand cell that had burned through our town was in Florida now, starting a new life, their memories wiped clean with a very intense siren formula. It had been nothing short of a massive undertaking: ninety-three-year-old siren tears, hair from a seal, the petal of a tulip, powdered pumpkin seeds, and many pomegranates. It had taken seventeen days to make, and the ingredients needed to be added at particular moments during the process. For example, one fresh pomegranate seed had to be added at the same time each day and a granule of powdered pumpkin seed had to be added every hour.

I guess it made sense that it was such a pain, considering it shouldn't be easy to completely wipe out someone's memory. Originally, they were going to be wiped to the first time Mr. Holmes had seen them at the truck stop, but then people started worrying about what brought them there in the first place.

I felt kind of bad for them—to be a stranger in a world they didn't remember, to have a life and no longer know it. Besides, what about their families? What if they had told someone about us? Riah's dad said Hand members often went missing, seeing as they were hunting abnormals who didn't usually think twice about disposing of such a threat, so it shouldn't arouse suspicion. And Ethan's uncle said that no one had come looking for them the weeks they'd been in our jail. They'd monitored surrounding papers and police reports and there had been no sign of concern.

We crossed the park, and Ethan hopped down onto the sandy area first, veered a few feet off the path, and reached down to pick up a little box. It was wood, with some scratchings on the sides that I couldn't decipher from where I was. He turned it in his hand and tried to open it, but when the top wouldn't release, he pulled his backpack around him and zipped it up safely inside.

"What is that?" I asked.

He shrugged. "I'll let you know when I get it open."

But some things didn't want to be opened, like Shady Woods. It was special and safe how it was, hiding and secret, protected by the forest and the gatekeepers. Protected by me.

As we entered the tree cover, where small patches of light landed on the path and underbrush like it had been sprinkled there, I realized this felt normal now: the trees, instead of buildings. The country instead of the city. The above-normal instead of the normal.

It was part of me, and I was home.

Book 2

The Little Wooden Box

Lined up on the counter was a baggie of dried seaweed, a paperclip, and an empty, shallow bowl.

I wasn't thinking a paperclip would feel so great going down and looked over at Christian to calm my nerves. He grabbed my hand and threw me a grin as his mom returned from the bathroom with a small jar of shimmering liquid. The silver flecks in her eyes were dull, drained, and she wasted no time pouring the contents of the jar into the bowl. Then she added a few pieces of seaweed.

With the contact, the siren tears began to pulse and create their own current, enveloping the seaweed and churning it to pieces.

Mrs. Riley waited for it to turn a shimmering green color before adding the paperclip, at which point the whole thing began to foam. Once the metal was thoroughly devoured, smoke started rising in curls from the center.

She turned to me. "Ready?"

I tried to force out an enthusiastic smile, but there was a paperclip in there.

She patted my shoulder and motioned toward the bowl. The liquid had not stopped moving.

"I drink it?" I asked, glancing over at Dr. Riley, who was at the sink. Surely a doctor wouldn't let me drink a paperclip.

Mrs. Riley grabbed a towel. "You breathe it in, Hon. It'll do the rest. Just lean your head over."

"And don't be alarmed, Grace. Let it do its thing." Christian squeezed my hand as I stepped away from him.

A sure way to alarm someone is to tell them not to be alarmed, but I wanted to see Iara—the watery underbelly of Shady Woods—and the only way to do that was through this bowl. So I squared my shoulders and looked down at the pulsating mini-ocean on the counter.

As I leaned over, I could have sworn it reached out for me. Jerking back, I eyed the liquid. "What exactly is it going to do?"

"I think it might be better if you aren't expecting it," Mrs. Riley said.

I didn't like the sound of that. But with a deep breath in, and final, unshakeable resolve, I closed my eyes and leaned all the way over. She laid a towel over my head, tenting me in with the microcosm, and I tried to relax with a very unsteady inhale.

The smoke came first, refreshingly cool vapors smelling of mint and sunshine, sending a chill all the way to my lungs. Then something more solid hit my nostrils.

I let out a garbled scream of surprise, and Christian's hand found my back. "It's okay," he whispered. "It won't hurt you."

I opened my eyes, but couldn't see much. The towel was lifted from my head. I tried to breathe in through my nose, but there was no longer a pathway there, filled as it was with the thick, live liquid that was now beginning its descent down my throat. It wasn't painful, just uncomfortable, and, quite frankly, scary as all get out. Good thing it worked on its own.

It took its time, easing its way at a slower rate than the smoke had, and then receded from my nose and airways. Like it had disappeared, only I could sort of feel the weight of it in my chest.

I stood up. "What's it doing? I mean, what does it do? How does it let me breathe underwater?"

"It coats the passageway," Mr. Riley explained. "And creates little pockets in your lungs so the water can't get through to the tissue, where it would do damage. Then it filters the oxygen out of the water and sends it through."

"Voila! And you now, my dear, can breathe under water!" Mrs. Riley swept the bowl from the counter and went to dump the remains in the sink. Not that there was much left.

"I think something's wrong with my eyes," I said. Everything had crisper edges, and the light was too bright, as if someone had flipped the switch when my eyes were already adjusted to the dark. I squinted until it stopped hurting.

"The smoke helps you see like us, too," Mrs. Riley explained. "Fun, right?"

I scanned the room and winced when my eyes hit the bright beams of sunlight shooting in through the window. "I didn't know sirens could see like this."

"Underwater it'll feel normal," Christian said. "Rather than cloudy and stuff like it does when you normally open your eyes in water."

"You said all you could do was breathe!" I cried. Christian was a dendrite, like his father and me, but apparently a little more siren than he let on.

He grinned and tugged me toward the basement stairs.

Also By J Mercer

More of the Shady Woods series

Shady Woods

The Little Wooden Box

Other young adult novels

Triplicity

Perfection and Other Illusive Things

Reviews really do make the world go round.
Please let others know what you thought!